LOUIS MARKOS

ILLUSTRATED BY ANGELA MERKLE

SILVERTON, OR

Lampion Press, LLC
P. O. Box 932
Silverton, OR 97381

ISBN: 978-1-942614-36-4

Library of Congress Control Number: 2017962203

Front Cover and Interior Illustrations by Angela Merkle

Cover Design and Text Formatting by Amy Cole, JPL Design Solutions

Printed in the United States of America

For Steve Rummelsburg

Who first loved these tales

BOOK 2 · IN THE SHADOW OF TROY

PART ONE: SAVING CIVILIZATION 1

Chapter One: Foundations 3
Chapter Two: The Golden Apple 9
Chapter Three: A Visit From an Old Friend......................... 17
Chapter Four: A Rather Unusual Flying Machine 25
Chapter Five: The Accuser.. 31
Chapter Six: The Land of Legend................................ 37
Chapter Seven: A View From the Tower 43
Chapter Eight: The Noble Enemy 55
Chapter Nine: Riddles in the Dark............................... 63

PART TWO: THE WRATH OF ACHILLES.................... 71

Chapter Ten: In the Tent of Achilles 73
Chapter Eleven: The Embassy 79
Chapter Twelve: The Counterfeit Achilles.................... 87
Chapter Thirteen: Creation and Destruction 97
Chapter Fourteen: Darkness at Noon.......................... 107
Chapter Fifteen: The Proper Way to Grieve 119
Chapter Sixteen: The Fall of Troy 131

PART THREE: FATHERS AND SONS 137

Chapter Seventeen: Longing for Home................................. 139
Chapter Eighteen: In the Cave of the Cyclops 147
Chapter Nineteen: The Curse Begins to Fall 155
Chapter Twenty: An Enchantress and a Prophet................. 161
Chapter Twenty-One: Dangers at Sea 171
Chapter Twenty-Two: Stepping Out of the Shadow........... 183
Chapter Twenty-Three: The Faithful and the Unfaithful... 197
Chapter Twenty-Four: The Marriage Bed............................ 211

THE GATES OF FREEDOM..219

About the Author 229
About the Illustrator.. 231

Sing to me, goddess, the wonderful tale of the marvelous children:
Brother and sister, chosen by fate for a task monumental,
Caught in the twisting, turning web of a struggle titanic,
Showed themselves fearless to stare in the face of an evil accuser.
Tell me Apollo and Artemis, siblings of Zeus and of Leto,
How did a burden so mighty fall on such delicate shoulders?
Was it the plan of the powers on high that our civilization,
Built on the tales of a hero of wrath and a hero of wisdom,
Carried by rhapsodes and poets, should totter so close to destruction?
Tell me it now from whatever the time and the place of its starting …

— Part —

1

Saving Civilization

"Oh men, your destiny.
When all is well a shadow can overturn it.
When trouble comes a stroke of the wet sponge,
And the picture's blotted out. And that,
I think that breaks the heart."
—Aeschylus

Foundations

One year had passed since Alex and Stacey had been carried back, by the magic of the dreaming stone and a set of pan-pipes, into the world of Greek mythology. As you might expect, they tried to tell their friends at school about their adventures, but nobody believed them. Still, their friends' unbelief didn't upset them as much as you might think. Their schoolmates loved to hear the tales, and, as a result, Alex (who was nine) and his sister, Stacey (who was eight), became quite popular at their school. Every time they went to the cafeteria for lunch or to the playground for recess, some eager young boy or girl was sure to ask them to tell again the story of how they rode on the back of the winged horse, Pegasus, or descended with Orpheus into the dark depths of Hades, or flew with the ill-fated Phaethon in the Golden Chariot of the Sun.

Alex and Stacey were always happy to oblige. Indeed, if the truth be told, Stacey never tired of telling her friends how she had helped Perseus slay the evil Medusa, while Alex was always quite willing to describe again how he had roped (Texas style) one of the horns of the Minotaur. Yes, for one whole year, Alex and Stacey were the center of attention at their school, and they gained a fine reputation for being excellent storytellers. Their teachers were particularly impressed. It had been a long time since they had taught children who knew *that* much about Greek mythology!

Still, even in the world of childhood, time has a way of pressing onward, and so, before Alex and Stacey knew it, the summer was upon them. Being ordinary children, they greeted this news with the appropriate response: yaaaaa-hooooo!

It was a hot and humid summer, even by Houston standards, but they didn't really mind. When they got too hot and sweaty playing outside, they would rush back indoors and watch a couple of hours of cartoons. When they had had enough of that, Stacey would lay down on an old blanket—really a sleeping bag—and order Alex to drag her round and round on the tile floor. Watching them play together, you never would have guessed that they had spent their previous summer fighting monsters and helping to rescue heroes and princesses.

Their father, who was an English Professor, also had the summer off, though he spent an awful lot of time in his office reading books and typing away on his computer. He was really very proud of his children and was happy to see what good storytellers they had become. Of course, he always made sure that Alex and Stacey learned as many different types of stories as they could. And so, when Daddy wasn't filling their heads with myths from ancient Greece, he was either reading them fairy tales from Hans Christian Andersen, the Brothers Grimm, and the Arabian Nights, or acting out for them the legends of Ireland, Japan, and India.

And always, always, there were the great heroes of the Bible: Abraham and Isaac, Jacob and Joseph, Moses and Joshua and David and Solomon. For the last six months or so, Daddy had taken Alex and Stacey on a whirlwind tour of the Old Testament from Adam and Eve to Daniel and Queen Esther. At first Alex closed his ears and said he was bored—he had, after all, heard most of the stories before in Sunday School—but Daddy found a way to make those old, old tales fresh and exciting. He told them the stories, not as they appeared in the Bible, but as if they were being told from God's point-of-view.

Well, that's all it took. From then on, you could hear a pin drop in Alex and Stacey's bedroom. They might have known the stories, but they had never heard them told like *that* before. Suddenly, like magic, all the tales fell together into a long and winding play— Daddy called it a "sacred drama." God, the author of the play, was trying to do something, to work out a plan that he had in his mind. But things kept going wrong. The people he loved and cared for kept turning away from him. Again and again God would rescue them and forgive them, but as soon as things got better, they would forget him again and run after their false gods. How those things caused pain to the heart of God! How he longed to hug his people and share their sorrow and joy!

Hearing the stories like that was like watching a man balanced on a tightrope that hung over a bottomless pit. Even the slightest slip could send him plummeting into the canyon below. How fragile it all was, like one of those little glass globes with the snowflakes in them that Alex liked to collect. It was all so beautiful and exciting, but a little bit frightening as well. For the history of the Jewish people was our history too. If their civilization ceased to exist, then so would ours. It was through the Jews that God prepared a plan that would one day reach out to include the whole world. And it all rested on a series of stories: of decisions made and unmade, wars lost and won, promises made and broken.

Thus had Alex and Stacey spent their evenings for the last six months. They had lived in the Bible stories with something close to the intensity and even the personal danger that had marked their adventures in the world of Greek mythology. There were times when they feared that the tightrope walker would fall, but somehow, he always regained his balance.

"Now, children," said Daddy, as Alex and Stacey laid their tired heads on their soft pillows and prepared for their bedtime story, "last night we finished our journey through the sacred drama of the Old Testament. Tonight, then, we will begin a new drama, one that may not be as sacred, but which is almost as important. For you see, children, for people like us who live in Europe or America, there are three books that must never be forgotten. The first is the Bible, and the second and third are the *Iliad* and *Odyssey*. We must never forget these great works, children, for they are the foundations of who and what we are."

"What's a foundation, Daddy?" asked Alex.

"Well, Alex," said Daddy, switching his voice so he sounded more like a teacher and less like a storyteller, "think of this house we live in. If you had x-ray vision and could look through the floor, you would see a thick slab of concrete stretching out in every direction. That slab is the foundation of our house, and on it rest the rooms, and the walls, and the ceiling. You can't see the foundation, and most of the time you forget it's there, but if you were to take it away or crack it in two, our entire house would collapse. Or think of your body. If you lost a hand or a leg or an ear, you could still survive. But if someone could reach down your throat and pull out your skeleton, your whole body would collapse into a quivering mass of jelly. Our skeleton is the foundation on which all the parts of our body rest."

"But Daddy, I don't understand what all that has to do with…"

"Now, now, Alex, let me finish"

(I probably don't have to remind you here that Daddy was a teacher and that teachers love to explain things slowly, one step at a time.)

"Just as the slab supports the weight of our house, and just as the skeleton holds together all the different parts of our body, so do the Bible, the *Iliad*, and the *Odyssey* provide us with all the laws and beliefs and virtues on which our civilization stands. If we are the tree, then they are the roots. The first tells us about the glory of God and of what we must do if we are to please him; the second and third tell us of the glory of man and of what it takes to be a hero. Together, they teach us what it means to be human, and it is only after we know that, that we can build a culture and a civilization that will last."

"Daddy," said Alex and Stacey together, "When are you going to tell us a story?" And then, because they had said the same thing at the same time, they quickly added:

"Jinx, personal jinx."

"Alright, children, alright," said Daddy, holding up his right hand and laughing. "But where shall I begin the story of the *Iliad*. That is to say, where shall I begin the story of Troy?"

"At the beginning, of course," said Stacey, who was getting a bit annoyed now by all the delays.

"Ah," said Daddy, and then rubbed his beard a few times, "that's not how Homer began. When he wrote his *Iliad*, he didn't start at the beginning but in the middle of things."

"Why would you start a story in the middle?" said Alex, slightly intrigued by such an illogical thought.

"Well, Alex, remember that airplane I gave you for your birthday? The one with the propeller attached to a thick, red rubber band? Before you could fly the plane, you had to twirl the propeller around and around. And each time you twirled it, the rubber band got thicker and thicker till it was a mass of twisty knots. If you waited until the knots were extra thick before you let the propeller go, the plane would stay in the air for a long time and would be sure to knock down something that Mommy didn't want knocked down. Of course if you got impatient and there were only a few knots in the rubber band, then when you let the airplane go it only stayed in the air for a couple of seconds. Homer started telling his story about Troy when the Trojan War had already been going on for nine years! That way, when he began, his story took off like a high-powered jet."

"Wow! That sounds cool, Daddy," said Alex.

"No, no, no," chimed in Stacey, who wasn't buying any of this, "I want to hear the story from the beginning."

"You mean you want to hear it 'from the egg?'"

"From the egg! Jinx, personal jinx!"

"Yes, when a Greek poet began from the beginning, he called it starting 'from the egg.' A chicken, after all, starts by being an egg. But, then again, that's not the only reason he called it starting 'from the egg.'"

"What was the other reason?" asked Stacey.

"That, children, I will tell you tomorrow."

"Oh, Dad," said Alex, but he knew it was useless. Zeus had spoken, and they would just have to wait until tomorrow to hear the start of the Trojan War.

The Golden Apple

Twenty-four hours passed quickly, and, before they knew it, Alex and Stacey were back in their beds, and Daddy was starting his tale:

"Once upon a time, the gods on Mount Olympus celebrated a wedding party. They invited all the gods and goddesses to attend—except one."

"That sounds just like Sleeping Beauty!" cried out Stacey, "I'll bet the one who wasn't invited got awfully mad."

"She certainly did, Stacey! Her name was Eris, which is the Greek word for discord or strife, and when she discovered that she was the only goddess who had not been invited, she swore that she would take her revenge. Now if she had been just a regular old goddess, she might have turned their food into dirty straw or started a rainstorm or put a pig's tail on the bride. But she was far from ordinary. She was the goddess of discord, after all, and she liked nothing better than making people angry and starting fights and wars and other nasty things. So she came up with a very clever and very sneaky plan.

"Using her magic powers, she took a piece of pure gold and shaped it into a beautiful, shiny apple. Then she engraved three words on the apple, "To the Fairest," and tossed the apple into the center of the party. Then she went back home and wasn't heard from again. Now the word "fairest" means "most beautiful," and so, when all the lovely goddesses who dwell on Mount Olympus with Zeus saw the apple and read the words, they all shouted that the apple should belong to them. Well, as you can imagine, there was a lot of screaming and a lot of discord, and a few of the goddesses, who didn't always act like ladies, even scratched and slapped some of the other goddesses.

"This went on for quite some time until finally, when all the dust settled and the screaming died down (believe me, children, some goddesses have *very* screechy voices), three goddesses stepped forward. Their names were Hera (HAIR ah), Athena (Ah THEE nah), and Aphrodite (a froh DIE tee), and all three of them absolutely refused to give up the apple. Now, if you remember your Greek mythology, then you will know that Hera was the wife of Zeus and thus the Queen of Olympus, Athena, one of Zeus's daughters, was the goddess of wisdom and of war, and Aphrodite, another daughter of Zeus, was the goddess of love. They were all as proud as they were beautiful, and no matter how much the guests begged them to back down, they all refused to budge. Instead, the three of them approached Zeus together and called on him to choose which of them was the fairest."

"I'll bet he chose Hera," said Stacey.

"No," chimed in Alex, "I think he chose Aphrodite."

"Well, children, you are both wrong. Remember, Zeus didn't become King of the Gods by being a fool. No, being the wise and crafty leader that he was, he simply answered: 'I think you are all pretty in your own way.' And I might add here, Alex, that when you grow up, it would be well for you if you remembered Zeus's answer. It might get you out of a tight spot with the ladies someday!

"But to return to our story, the goddesses were not satisfied with Zeus's answer, and so they went, one by one, to all the other gods on Olympus seeking a judgment as to who was the fairest. But no one would choose. You see, all three of those goddesses were very powerful, and no one wanted to anger two of them by making the other one happy. Having goddesses as your enemies is really not good business.

"Finally, in desperation, the goddesses left Mount Olympus and flew down to the earth. Perhaps there they could find a mortal man who would decide for them who deserved the apple. After a long search, they came upon a shepherd lying on a mountaintop in the hills behind the mighty city of Troy. The name of the mountain was Ida (EYE dah) and the name of the shepherd was Paris. He was a very handsome lad and could be a good fighter when he wanted to be, but he was also a bit lazy and vain, and there were times when he only seemed to care about himself.

"When Paris saw the three goddesses suddenly appear on the ground in front of him, he jumped up in excitement and stood on tiptoe. But, being the lazy fellow that he was, he quickly tired of standing up like that and leaned over on his shepherd's staff instead. He stared and stared at the three lovely women; in all his life, he had never seen anything so beautiful.

"'Paris,' they said sweetly, 'You must choose which of us is the fairest. Only you, young man, are wise and handsome enough to decide. Please now, O mortal, make your choice.'

"Paris licked his lips a couple of times and then walked closer. For a few moments, he thought that he must surely be dreaming. But, no, it was really happening. These three visions of loveliness wanted him to be their judge. Of course, I use that word 'judge' very loosely. None of those three proud goddesses was looking for a truly fair judge. Each of them only wanted one thing: to have the Golden Apple.

"And so, one by one, the three goddesses brushed close to Paris and whispered in his ear a tempting bribe:

"'Choose me,' said Hera, 'and I will make you a great and wealthy King.'

"'Choose me,' said Athena, 'and I will make you the greatest warrior who ever lived.'

"'Choose me,' said Aphrodite, 'and I will give you the most beautiful woman in the world as your wife.'"

"Which one did he choose?" asked Alex.

"Well, Paris was young …"

"Yes."

"And he was foolish …"

"Yes."

"He chose Aphrodite. And by doing so, he made two terrible enemies. From then on, Hera and Athena not only hated Paris, but they hated Troy as well."

"Why did they hate Troy?" asked Stacey, "That doesn't seem fair."

"Because you see, children, Paris was not really a shepherd. He was none other than the son of Priam (PRY am), King of Troy. Priam had heard a prophecy that Paris would cause the destruction of his city, and so Paris had been sent away to live on Mount Ida. But he was still by blood a prince of Troy and brother to the high Prince and first-born son of Priam: the great Hector. His decision to choose Aphrodite led in the end to the death of his brother, his father, and his whole glorious city."

"I guess he should have told the goddesses that they were all pretty in their own way."

"Exactly, Alex! But then, of course there wouldn't be a story if he had. And that story has to do with the bribe offered to him by Aphrodite. Yes, he would have the most beautiful woman in the world as his wife—the goddess hadn't lied—but he would have to steal her away from her husband. Because, as you will also learn when you get older, Alex, if you should ever find the most beautiful woman in the world, she will most likely be married to someone else."

"Daddy?"

"What is it, Alex?"

"I think I know who the girl was that Paris took away."

"Who?"

"Helen of Troy."

"Exactly right! But at this point in the story she wasn't a Trojan but a Greek from the city of Sparta."

"Sparta," said Alex and Stacey together (they were too excited to remember to follow that with "Jinx, personal jinx"), "that's where our relatives live, where we stayed last summer. Was the most beautiful woman in the world really a Spartan?"

"Yes, she was," said Daddy with pride, "She was the daughter of a lovely girl named Leda (LEE da), but her father was not the husband of Leda. Her father, children, was none other than Zeus himself. The King of the Gods looked down one day from Mount Olympus, and when he saw Leda, he fell in love with her instantly. Not wanting to come to her in the form of a god or a man, he chose to appear in the form of a swan. And so, when it came time for Leda to have her baby, she gave birth, not to a child, but to a large white egg. At first, she didn't know what to do, but then, with a sharp crack, the egg split open and out popped baby Helen."

"The egg, the egg," cried Stacey with delight, "that's the egg. That's what it means to start from the egg. To start when Helen was born."

"Exactly right, Stacey! You have a good memory. It was that very egg that started the whole long tale of the Trojan War. When Helen grew up, she was so beautiful that all the Kings of Greece fought to take her for their wife. Fearing a war would take place, Leda's husband invited them all to his castle for a contest. The winner of the contest, he said, would marry Helen and take her home to be his queen. But even that was not enough. Before the contest began, all the kings were forced to take an oath that they would protect the rights of whichever one of them won the contest. That is to say, if Helen were ever stolen away from the winner of the contest, all the other kings would band together and fight to get her back.

"And so the contest was held, and the winner was Menelaus (men a LAY us), the noble son of an old hero named Atreus (AY tree us). Well, children, maybe you can guess what happened next. Once Paris learned about Helen he got on a boat and sailed across the Aegean (a GEE en) Sea to Sparta. Menelaus, being a good host, as all Greeks are supposed to be, took Paris into his home and gave him lots of food to eat and lots of presents to take home with him to Troy. But Paris paid back his host with treachery. That very night, while everyone in the castle was asleep, he stole Helen away and sailed with her back to Troy.

"The next morning, when Menelaus discovered what had happened he called on all the Kings of Greece to hold true to their promise. They gathered on the eastern coast of the Aegean with all their troops and their ships and prepared to sail for Troy. You would think that Menelaus would lead the expedition, but since his brother, Agamemnon (a ga MEM non) was the richest of the kings and had the most ships, he was chosen to be the commander-in-chief.

"And so it was that on a fateful day over three thousand years ago, a mighty war began that is still remembered today, a war that changed everything and that taught the world what it truly means to be a hero."

With that, Daddy stood up and tucked Alex and Stacey in nice and tight. Then, as he always did after he finished telling his story, he prayed that they would have a good night sleep without any nightmares and that no monsters or goblins or ghosts would bother them while they slept. It was a prayer that God had always answered before. But this night would be just a little bit different...

A Visit From an
Old Friend

"Stacey," whispered Alex, after Daddy had gone back downstairs, "Did you notice something interesting about the story Daddy told us tonight?"

"What, Alex?"

"The apple, Stacey, the apple."

"What about it?"

"Well, when Daddy told us the Bible stories, they started with an apple too: the one that Adam and Eve ate in the Garden of Eden."

"You're right. I wonder if it's important. Do you think it has to do with those "boundations" that Daddy told us about last night?"

"That's FOUN-dations, Stacey."

"That's what I said."

"No you didn't."

"Yes, I…"

"It doesn't matter, Stacey, because I think you're right. I think it *does* have to do with foundations. It's like two different stories that have the same beginning. Maybe they have the same ending too. Daddy *did* say that both stories were important, that one tells us how to obey God and the other one how to be a hero."

"We certainly met a lot of heroes last year: Perseus and Orpheus and Theseus. Do you think we'll ever get a chance to meet more heroes?"

"I don't know, Stacey. There must be something different about the heroes of the Trojan War, but I can't figure out what it is. Daddy seemed more serious when he was talking about the *Iliad* and the *Odyssey*. Do you think …"

But he never got a chance to finish his thought. For at that very moment, both Alex and Stacey heard a bumping sound coming from Stacey's closet. Now, you need to understand that Stacey's closet was a little bit different than most closets. If you opened it up and looked inside, it would seem at first glance to be a regular closet, with clothes hanging down from a rod that stretched from one end of the closet to the other. But if you put your head in and looked to the right, you would see, not a wall, as you would in most closets, but a little alcove. And in that alcove—you might call it a cubby hole—was what looked like a big stair or seat covered with a thick carpet.

Well, let me rephrase myself. That's what you *would* have seen if Stacey's closet hadn't been absolutely stuffed with blankets and animals and toys. Actually, to be quite honest, there was so much stuff in the closet that you couldn't even close the door all the way. But that's how Stacey liked it. Whenever she was sad or angry or just wanted to be alone, she would climb into her closet, burrow under all the thick blankets, and sit on the little stair inside the alcove.

And it was precisely from that alcove that the bumping sound was coming.

"What was that sound?" said Stacey, "Did you put something in my closet, Alex?"

"No, Stacey, I didn't put anything in there. Why don't you go look in the closet?"

"I'm not going anywhere near that closet. What if it's a rat or a giant spider? You go and look, Alex. I'll wait here, and if something grabs you, I'll run downstairs and get Mommy."

"Thanks a lot, Stacey. That makes me feel a whole lot better. Well, I guess I better go look. But hand me my pirate sword first. And you better give me my walking stick too, the one we got when we went camping."

And so, with his sword in one hand and his stick in the other, Alex bravely made his way toward the closet. He tried to remember how he had felt last year when he was helping out the heroes of Greek mythology, but it didn't make him feel any less scared. Still, he didn't want his sister to think he was afraid, and so, step by step, he moved his slightly shaky legs closer to the closet.

When he was only about four feet away from the door—which was already cracked open a bit due to the mess—he reached out his walking stick and touched it to the inside of the door. Then, by carefully pushing the stick to the left, he forced open the door. When he did this, the bumping sound got a bit louder and a pale green light glowed from within the closet.

Alex moved a few steps closer and then bent his back forward until his head came close to the opening of the door. To his surprise, he saw something long and skinny poking out of the area where the alcove was.

"Don't worry, Stacey," said Alex with a sigh of relief, "it's just that big stuffed snake that I got in Florida."

Alex, after laying down his stick and sword, reached out and took a hold of it, expecting it to feel soft and fluffy. But it didn't feel soft *or* fluffy. It was hard and a little bit slippery.

"Hey, wait a minute …"

For the second time that night, Alex didn't finish his sentence. The thing in his hand, as if it were a rope being pulled, moved suddenly and quickly toward the alcove. And Alex, who was too shocked to let go, was dragged in along with it.

"Alex!" screamed Stacey, and ran toward the closet. I suppose she should have run downstairs and gotten Mommy, but she wasn't going to leave her brother alone. Like a mermaid diving into the ocean, she leaped into the closet and burrowed under the blankets. Two seconds later she pulled herself up on to the seat in the alcove, only to find it occupied already by something very hairy. Without thinking, she grabbed a tuft of hair in each hand and pulled with all her might. A scream that was not exactly human but not exactly animal rang out from the alcove, and Alex, Stacey, and something else came tumbling out of the closet.

As soon as they regained their balance, Alex and Stacey jumped to their feet and looked down at the something else—which looked like nothing else they had ever seen. Or had they? From the waist up it looked like a hairy little man, but from the waist down it looked like a goat. It had two horns on its head, two hooves instead of feet, and a long, dark tail that stretched from behind it like a snake. Or did it? As they watched in wonder, the tail began to shrink, until it was short and stubby like the tail of a goat.

"Oh my gosh, it's Pan. Jinx, personal jinx!"

"Well, children, I hope I haven't come all this way to have a jinx put on me. Things are bad enough as they are without having to add on more bad luck. I thought I was going to suffocate in that closet. Your father certainly likes to tell long stories."

I suppose I should break in here and tell you that Pan was a satyr (SAY ter) and that he was indeed half man and half goat. In the ancient days of Greece, Pan lived in the woods and watched over the trees and the fields and the animals. Most of the time, he was friendly, but sometimes he would go wild and do a dance that turned everything topsy-turvy. On days like that, he could be really quite scary and cause a panic in any village that he came near. In fact, our word "panic" comes from the name Pan.

When Alex and Stacey had visited Greece the year before, they had met Pan in the fields. He had taught them to listen to the music of the forest and to do the dance of the wind, and then had promptly disappeared, leaving behind a gift for Alex: a set of pan-pipes. It was that set of pipes, together with Stacey's dreaming stone, that had allowed the children to enter, by magic, into the world of Greek mythology.

"Pan," said Alex, "How did you get here?"

"Well, I'm not rightly sure, my boy. After I was told of the danger and how important it was that I find you and your sister, I stood in the center of the forest and began to spin. I spun faster and faster, and as I did my tail began to grow and wrapped itself around and around my waist. The next thing I knew I was in your closet."

"Danger?" said Stacey, "Did you say something about danger?"

"Yes, my dear, I did say danger."

"But who's in danger?" broke in Alex, "Is someone chasing you, Pan?"

"No, no, it's not me who's in danger. It's you, all of you, your whole civilization, maybe even your whole world. That's why I've come back to get you. There's an evil loose in our world, and it's trying to destroy the Trojan War."

"How can you destroy a war?" asked Alex.

"Well, it's not exactly the war that the evil is trying to destroy. It's everything about the war: the heroes and the heroines and all the things they did and said and chose."

"But why should that put *us* in danger?"

"Don't you see. If you change the war, if you strip it of its heroes and all the decisions made by those heroes, then you change the *Iliad* and *Odyssey* as well. Homer didn't just make up his epic poems. He based them on the stories of the Trojan War and of the Greeks who returned home after the war was over. Without those stories, Homer would not have written, or, worse yet, he would have written something very different: darker, less heroic, less human."

"I still don't under ..."

"Children, if you take away Homer you take away the whole foundation of your civilization."

"Oh!" said Alex and Stacey together, when they heard Pan use the word foundation. It was as if someone had hit them suddenly in the chest, and they had woken up out of a deep sleep. They had felt afraid when they first heard the bump in the closet, but now they felt a different kind of fear, a cold kind of dread that made something flutter inside of them.

Pan, who could see that the truth was dawning in their eyes, grabbed a hold of their hands and pulled them closer to him:

"I see you are beginning to understand. That is good. I do not have time to explain any more. We must leave at once. Go get the dreaming stone and the panpipes. We must not delay any longer … What are you waiting for, children? Get them now!"

"But, but, we can't, Pan," said Alex quietly, "When we returned home, the stone and the pipes disappeared. They are gone. It's like they never existed."

"Then we are all lost."

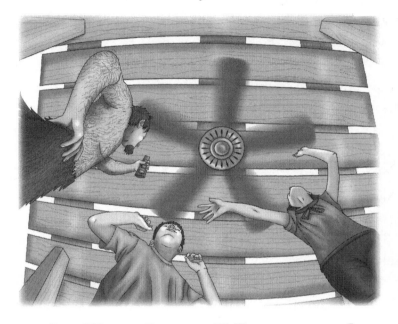

A Rather Unusual Flying Machine

For several minutes, no one moved and no one spoke. Then, slowly, Pan began to pace back and forth across the room.

"It cannot be. It *cannot* be. I would not have been sent if I could not return with the children. There must be a way." Then, stopping and looking directly at Alex, he said: "My boy, do you have something we can use to fly in? Some winged slippers or a flying horse or maybe a chariot that we can yoke to the horses of the sun?"

"We don't have things like that in our world. There is no magic here."

"No, Alex," shouted Stacey. "That's not true! Don't you remember what Daddy taught us: 'The world is full of magic: you just have to have eyes to see it and ears to hear it.'"

"Yes, my dear," said Pan, "You speak wisely. We must use our eyes and our ears. We must *find* the magic for ourselves. Quick, look around you."

Like two bloodhounds in search of an escaped criminal, Alex and Stacey sniffed out every inch of their house—at least the upstairs; they were afraid if they went downstairs, they would wake up Mommy and Daddy. They tried as hard as they could to find the magic, but there was just no magic to be found.

"Don't give up, children," said Pan, "Open your eyes. Think. Think. Where haven't we looked yet?"

"The window!" cried Stacey, "We haven't looked outside yet."

Immediately, Alex and Stacey rushed to the window and looked out over their backyard.

"Nothing out there," said Alex, "Nothing but the deck, I mean."

"Deck?" asked Pan, "Describe this deck for me."

"It was built by one of our Daddy's friends. It's very strong, made out of the best wood. Let's see. It's about sixteen feet long and another sixteen feet wide. I think it's raised about two feet off of the ground with a big step running all the way around it. At first Daddy was going to leave it open on the top, but then he and his friend decided to cover part of it. So they chose one corner of the deck and attached four long wooden poles. Then they joined together the four poles and built a roof. But it's not an ordinary roof. You can see through it. But my favorite part is that right in the center of the roof, they put in a fan with a light on it."

"You describe it well," said Pan. "Now tell me, how high up is the fan?"

"Oh, it's pretty high. Even if I stood on my Daddy's shoulders I couldn't touch it. It must be over ten feet high. That's why we have a remote control to turn on the light and fan."

"Yes," Pan muttered to himself, stroking his rough little beard, "It just might work." Then in a louder voice, he said: "Children, put on your clothes. We must go outside at once. Don't worry about making noise: I will put a sleeping spell on your parents and your neighbors. Come, we must be swift!"

A few minutes later, Alex, Stacey, and Pan were standing outside on the deck. Alex was holding the remote control tightly in his hand; he had already turned on the light.

"Alright, Alex," said Pan, "Turn on the fan!"

Alex pushed the first fan button, and the blades of the fan began to spin.

"Can't you make it go any faster than that?"

Alex pushed the second fan button, and the blades began to spin faster.

"C'mon, boy, faster I tell you."

Alex pushed the third button, and the fan whipped around in the night air. He could feel the wind it made in his hair and on his face.

"No, no that will never do. Can't you make it go any faster?"

"But Pan," said Alex, "that's as fast as it goes. There are no more buttons."

"Give me that contraption, boy; maybe I can find another button."

Alex gave it to him and Pan began spinning it around and around in his hands. "Ah ha," he said after a few minutes, "I *knew* it."

With a strange little twist of his hands, Pan popped open a compartment in the back of the remote control—a secret compartment which Alex and Stacey had never seen before and which they could never find again. Inside the compartment was a little button shaped like a star. Pan pushed it, and as soon as he did, the blades of the fan began to hum like the propellers of a jet. Faster and faster they spun, until Alex and Stacey could no longer see them. They were just a blur. The wind from the fan was so strong now that Pan and the children had to grab the wooden poles and hold on with all of their strength.

And still the blades spun faster.

Two minutes after Pan pushed the star-shaped button, the floor of the deck began to shake. Two minutes later, the ground *under* the deck began to shake as well, and the poles began to sway like palm trees in a hurricane.

"I can't hold on any longer," cried Stacey, but no one heard her. For the very moment she said it, the stillness of the evening was shattered by the sound of a terrifying crack. Underneath their feet, Pan and the children could hear and feel the vibrations of wood beams being ripped in half. The deck was being torn apart. The fan continued to increase in speed and power so that now it was pulling up and away from the deck like a hot air balloon fighting against the ropes that would hold it down.

Both Alex and Stacey screamed, and, just as they did, the whole deck ripped itself out of the ground and soared upward into the air. Higher and higher it rose, pulled skyward by the furious twisting of the blades. The children held their breath and wrapped their legs as well as their arms around the wooden poles. It was both the scariest and most exciting moment they had ever experienced.

"Eeeee-hawwwww!" yelled Alex, in his very best Texas accent. "I'll bet no cowboy ever rode a bucking bronco like this before. How are you doing, Stacey?"

"I'm still holding on, Alex, but don't ask me to look down."

For several more minutes, the deck continued to climb into the air, pawing and snorting like a stallion as it fought the crushing force of gravity. It was a wild ride, but, in the end, the deck won; and Alex and Stacey, to their great relief, felt the deck slow to a halt and then begin to hover gently in the air. They let go of the poles and sank slowly to the floor of the deck. They no longer felt like astronauts in a rocket; now they felt more like passengers on a ship sailing smoothly over a calm ocean. Needless to say, it was a very nice feeling.

"Next stop, Troy," said Pan, as if he were the conductor on a train.

"Oh, boy, Stacey," said Alex, "I think we're in for quite a summer!"

The Accuser

For at least an hour, neither Alex nor Stacey nor Pan said a single word. The view from the deck was so beautiful, so breathtaking that no one wanted to speak or even breathe. If you've ever been on an airplane, you will know how strange and exciting it is when your plane flies through a bank of clouds and everything becomes white for miles and miles. Well, that's sort of how Alex and Stacey felt, except for the fact that what they were flying through were not clouds but stars.

The stars glittered and shone around them like a million fireflies on a warm July evening. Stacey stretched out her arms and caught some of the "star stuff" in her hands. It was very cold and very delicate and had blue veins running through it. Had Stacey been from up North, she would have thought that it looked like snow, but since she was from Houston, Texas—where it never snows, even at Christmas—she thought instead that it looked like fairy dust. After holding it for a second, she threw it back in to the sky. It jumped out of her hands and began to spin. As it spun, it made a sound that was partly like steam escaping from a teapot and partly like a baby laughing. Stacey couldn't help but laugh along.

Now I suppose that some of you are asking yourselves how Alex and Stacey could possibly breathe if they were high enough up to see the stars. Well, that was perhaps the most wonderful part of all. As the fan spun round and round, it produced not only wind, but air: real air that you could breathe. And the air, which was lit up by the light bulb that hung from the fan, was warm, warm enough to protect all three of them from the coldness of space.

Picture if you will two actors and one actress standing on a dark stage. Suddenly, someone turns on a spotlight that shines down from the ceiling and completely encircles the actors. All around them it is still dark, but within the glowing circle all is bright. That's exactly how Alex, Stacey, and Pan looked as they huddled together on the floor of the deck. The air from the fan, lit by the bulb, formed itself into a spinning cone, and as long as they remained inside that cone, they could breathe and see and stay warm.

"Well, children," said Pan, breaking the long silence, "soon we will arrive in Troy. Once we are there, I shall take you first within the walls where you will meet the Trojans: Priam and his wife Hecuba (HECK you ba) and their two sons, Hector and Paris. There too you shall meet their daughter, Cassandra (Ka SAN dra), and their lovely daughters-in-law, Andromache (an DRA ma key), wife of

Hektor, and Helen, wife of Paris. After that, we shall move outside the walls where you will meet the heroes of Greece."

"But, Pan," said Alex, "You still haven't explained to us what the danger is. What is this evil force that you told us about in our bedroom?"

"The evil one has no name, my son, but we have learned to call him 'the Accuser.'"

"But I thought the bad guy was Hades (HAY dees), the King of the Underworld."

"No, Alex. I can't say that I particularly care for Hades, but he is not what I would call evil. He has a job to do, and sometimes he does it with a little too much enthusiasm, but it is his job nonetheless. He is lonely and complains a lot, and sometimes he can be angry or even cruel, but he is not evil in the way that the Accuser is evil."

"Well," said Stacey, "I can't say that I like Hades either, especially after he stole Persephone (per SEF oh nee) away from her mother, Demeter (De MEE ter). But, I guess he did it because he loved her, and if he could really love her, then perhaps he is not all evil."

"Well put, little one," said Pan, "I have studied you humans for many years now. Very few of you really understand what evil is. You call war evil or getting drunk evil or stealing evil. But these things are only symptoms of a much greater disease. I've even heard you humans say that having fun is evil. What a silly thought! Evil, true evil, is the very opposite of fun. It is cold and miserable and empty. Evil is a thief, but he doesn't steal money or jewelry or cars. He steals life and joy and hope and peace."

"But why does he do that?" asked Stacey innocently.

"Why? Who knows why? All I know is that he hates every-thing that is good or noble or heroic. He is anti-everything. We call him the Accuser because he crawls into the ears of our greatest warriors and whispers to them that they are worthless. He tells them that virtue means nothing and that rules and codes and oaths are for cowards and fools.

Once he even appeared to the young Hercules and tried to tempt him away from the path chosen for him by the gods. He disguised himself as a tall and beautiful woman dressed in fine clothes and met the hero at a crossroads. There, he promised Hercules that if he followed him—or her; one can never trust the Accuser— he would have an easy life and get all the things he wanted right away without having to work or wait for them. She stared boldly at Hercules as she spoke, and the hero could see that her face was painted with unnatural colors and that her lips were like those of a hungry lion.

"Suddenly, there appeared beside Hercules a second woman, but this one was truer and more pure than the disguised Accuser. She wore a white robe and held a staff in her hand. She seized Hercules by the hair and told him to beware of the false woman and to choose instead the path of virtue. That path would be longer and would call for hard work and even some suffering, but if he followed it, he would gain honor throughout Greece. He would reap the reward that he himself sowed with his own hands.

"'No!' cried the Accuser, 'Don't listen to her, Hercules. If you follow her road, you will have to wait many years for your reward. Follow me, and you shall have joy and pleasure without toil or study or exercise.'

"'Wretched woman,' replied the Lady in White, 'what do you know of joy or pleasure or reward? Before you are even hungry, you devour your food, and before you feel the slightest thirst, you gorge yourself with wine. You sleep when you are not tired and bathe when you are not dirty. Because you do not enjoy what you have, you take more, but as soon as you take it, you despise it. Those who follow you are left empty and dry. The small pleasure you give them sucks the life out of them and makes them hated by their friends and rejected by their families. No, Hercules, reject her offer and take the high road of virtue ...'"

"Well," said Stacey, "Well. Which did he choose?"

"Which did he choose? Which did he choose? We are speaking of Hercules, my girl! He who saved all Greece from the monsters and fiends that would destroy us. He who killed the Hydra (HIGH dra) and the Nemean (na MEE en) Lion and the terrible man-eating birds. He who captured and tamed countless wild beasts and even kidnapped Cerberus (SIR ba rus) himself, the three-headed dog of Hades. He who, when he died, was taken up to dwell on Mount Olympus with the gods. What did he choose, indeed! No sooner did the Lady in White finish her speech than Hercules lifted his club and brought it down squarely on the head of the Accuser."

"So then, the Accuser must be dead," said Alex with a hopeful smile.

"Alas, it is not so easy to destroy evil. For many years the Accuser lay in a dreamless sleep, buried deep in the earth by the force of Hercules' club. But now he has returned, and his hatred of all virtue has grown stronger. He even comes before Zeus, when he dares, and slanders the heroes that Zeus most loves."

"But why?" said Stacey again, "Why?"

"Have you children never heard the proverb: misery loves company? Well, the Accuser is miserable, and he would spread his misery throughout all Greece, throughout the whole world if he could. Haven't you ever met a spoiled and miserable child who would rather break his toys than let the other children play with them? This is the Accuser with whom you must deal."

When Alex heard that bit about breaking other children's toys, his blood rose to his face, and he began to clench his fists. "Pan," he said, in a deep and strong voice, "show me where this Accuser is. I want to punch him right in the nose."

"Ah, yes, you are Hercules reborn! I knew my mission would not be in vain. But you cannot defeat an enemy like this with your fists. You can only defeat him as the Lady in White defeated him, by speaking a better message and a better promise. You must stand beside the heroes of Greece and of Troy and remind them of the way of virtue. You must enter into their struggles and share in their joys. You may even have to suffer alongside them. You must remind them *what* they are and *who* they are: that they are special, that they are valuable, that they were made for a purpose."

"When do we start, Pan?" asked Stacey.

"Yes, yes, your brother shall be Hercules, and you shall be the Lady in White. Through you two the Accuser *will* be defeated. But come, even now I see the Walls of Troy towering up before us. Our journey has ended. We have arrived."

The Land of Legend

P an was right. When Alex and Stacey bent forward, and looked down over the edge of the deck, they saw spreading out below them a low-lying hill. On top of the hill was a city that hung on the mountaintop like an eagle perched on a crag. Around the city, there ran a thick, high wall made of huge stones piled one upon the other. It reminded the children of the great walls they had seen the year before at Mycenae (my SEE nee), walls that, according to legend, had been built by the giant Cyclopes. Much of the wall was tilted forward slightly, and it seemed to Alex that if someone ran very, very fast, he might just be able to run up the side of the wall.

But Stacey didn't notice that part. She was looking instead at the two watchtowers that were built into the wall and that shot upward into the sky. They had flat roofs, and she could see groups of people standing on the roofs and talking to one another. At times, they would look out, away from the city, on to a large grassy plain. Normally, the plain would have been peaceful, and horses would have been grazing on it, but now the plain was a-flurry with activity.

A massive army was camped on the plain. Stacey could see their tents and fires stretched out along the beach for miles and miles. As it was early evening, there was no actual fighting going on, but she could see soldiers practicing with their swords and spears, while others wheeled around in chariots pulled by fierce war horses. As she stared and stared at the amazing sight below her, the deck suddenly veered down and away and landed behind Troy on the side opposite to the grassy plain. Pan and the children stepped off of the deck and walked over to the wall. As Alex looked up toward the top of the nearest watchtower, the evening sun shifted and cast a long, dark shadow over the three of them.

"I can't believe I'm standing here in the shadow of the famous Trojan Wall!"

"Ah, my boy, not just you but your whole civilization stands in the shadow of Troy. The game we play today is a game played for high stakes. Let us pray we do not fail."

"But how will we ever get in the city?" asked Alex.

"Don't worry about that, young Hercules. The trees and the water and the earth are all at my command. All alike must answer to my pipes."

With those words, Pan stretched out his hand, and a set of panpipes magically appeared in his fingers. He blew gently over the tops of the pipes, and a melody like the sound of sap running up a tree or worms burrowing through the earth rose upward and wrapped itself around the children. The music grew louder and faster, and Alex and Stacey felt a rumbling beneath their feet.

I'm sure most of you have watched water run down a drain after you have finished taking your bath. The best part, of course, is right near the end, when the water forms into a little whirlpool and swirls swiftly around as it disappears into the dark pipe. Well, the children saw something like that now, but the whirlpool that formed was not made of water but of earth. Round and round the dirt swirled until, with a fierce snap like the breaking of a hundred tree roots, the ground near their feet opened up and sucked in the dirt. And with the dirt, it sucked in Pan and the children as well!

What Alex and Stacey felt next was very similar to the feeling one has when one goes shooting down a water slide. This slide was a bit bumpier and considerably more muddy than the ones you go on at an amusement park, but it was thrilling none the less. And the dirt didn't matter much, since the slide ended with a cold, wet plunge into an underground river.

"Why have you taken us here, Pan?" said Alex after he had gotten back his voice. "Now we're farther than ever from getting into Troy."

"On the contrary, Alex, we are much closer than you think. This river lies directly under the palace of King Priam. It is this river, in fact, that has helped the Trojans to survive for so long. That Greek army has been camped out there for nine years now, and they have tried their best to cut off the Trojans from all supplies of food and water. But they have been unsuccessful. Priam is a wise king, and he knows many tricks for surviving a siege. This river is one of them. It supplies the palace and the city with fresh, clean water. Soon, Priam and his family will go to sleep. When that time comes, we shall climb up the staircase on the other side of the river and sneak our way into the palace. For now, let us eat and drink. Here is all the water we need, and I know where the Trojans have hidden some food in case of an emergency."

While Pan went in search of the food, Alex, who was quite a good Boy Scout, gathered some twigs and built a fire. Not until they began to drink some water from the river did they realize how very thirsty they were. And the food, once it was cooked on the fire, tasted better than any food they had eaten in a long, long time. For about ten minutes, they all ate in silence, but, once their bellies were full enough to stop them from grumbling and growling, Alex looked up at Pan and asked him a question that had been bothering him for the last few hours:

"Pan, last year we met and helped the heroes of Greek mythology. This year in school, we studied about the heroes of history and all their great deeds. But these heroes we are about to meet, what are they? Are they myths or are they historical?"

"Neither, my boy … and both. This land to which your deck has carried us is the land of legend. It lies midway between the world of myth and the world of history. It is the place where noble ideas are born and heroic deeds are wrought. Like the heroes of myth, the heroes of legend are larger than life and their strength is past counting; but, like the heroes of history, their actions and their choices have a direct effect on all that comes after them. Unlike the world of myth, the land of legend can be assigned a date and a year on the calendar: in case you are wondering, Alex, it is now roughly 1250 BC. And yet, unlike the world of history, the land of legend lies equally far from every age that comes after it. Homer was just as far from, and just as close to, the Trojan War as those who would be born a thousand years later or two thousand years later, or, like you and your sister, over three thousand years later."

"I understand!" said Alex, "It's just like the stories of King Arthur and the Round Table."

"Hmm," thought Pan, "I do not know this King of whom you speak, but I can see by your eyes that you understand. But come, by now the palace must be asleep. It is time that we made our way into the heart of Troy."

A View From the Tower

The palace of Priam was quite different than Alex and Stacey had expected. Yes, it was very large and very fancy with golden shields hanging from the walls and beautiful statues and vases lying everywhere. Still, for all its glory and richness, it felt somehow like a home.

Pan and the children had come out into a courtyard planted with the most colorful and delicate flowers that Stacey had ever seen, and there were fountains of every size hidden among them. Winding pathways made of smooth stones ran in and out among the fountains and flowers, and the song of a dozen nightingales filled the air with a delicious sound that mingled with the even more delicious smell of the flowers. Along both sides of the courtyard were bedchambers made of marble and connected together by a network of passages. On one side ran fifty chambers, each of which housed one of the brave sons, and one of the lovely daughters-in-law, of Priam. Along the other ran twelve chambers, each of which housed one of the lovely daughters, and one of the brave sons-in-law, of Priam.

"I wish I could live in a palace like this," said Stacey, "It's so beautiful and peaceful ..."

But that's all that Stacey said. The sound of the nightingales and of the water splashing in the fountains made both Stacey and Alex feel terrible sleepy. With a big yawn, they both lied down on a patch of grass in the middle of the courtyard and promptly fell into a deep sleep.

They were wakened several hours later by a pair of hands shaking them gently:

"Wake up you silly children," said a friendly voice, "This is no place to sleep. You'll catch your death of cold."

Alex and Stacey woke up to find themselves surrounded by people dressed in togas. Some were stretching and running in place; others were doing somersaults and complicated dance steps; yet others were sitting on the ground telling stories to a whole assortment of children. Servants in different colored togas moved among them: some carrying water; some cleaning the stones; some tending to the flowers. Alex and Stacey looked all around the courtyard in search of Pan, but he was nowhere to be seen. Then they looked at each other, and found to their surprise that they were dressed in togas as well.

"Come, children," said the friendly voice again, "You must be starving. I was just about to feed my baby, Astyanax (a STY a nax). Why don't you join us for breakfast?"

"Thank you, ma'am," said Alex, not knowing what else to say. The lady was tall and very pretty, and both of the children liked her immediately. Her smile was warm and honest and her voice like music. She only had one baby, but she seemed the type of lady who could have ten children and still look as young and strong and pretty as when she had her first. But she also seemed strangely troubled. Around her eyes there were tiny lines and circles, as if she had spent long days and nights watching for someone who never came. Her laugh was beautiful, but underneath the laugh there was trouble as well. It was as if she laughed not only because she was happy but because she knew that if she didn't laugh, she would start to cry and never stop.

Alex and Stacey followed her to her chamber—it was the first chamber and also the biggest—and quickly ate whatever she put before them. They were really quite hungry. When they had finished, the lady asked them their names. Normally, they would have said Alex and Stacey, but they felt so formal dressed in their togas, that they used their full names instead: Alexander and Anastasia.

"Alexander?" said the lady with a smile, "Why, that's my brother-in-law's name. Yes, to most of the world he is known as Paris, but here in Troy we call him Alexander as well."

"You are the sister-in-law of Paris?" said Stacey with amazement, "Then you must know his wife, Helen. I wish that we could meet Helen. I've heard that she's the most beautiful woman in the world."

"Well," said the lady, "I suppose I really should take you two home to your mother, but you seem like such nice children that I will take you right now to see Helen. She is up on the watchtower with my father-in-law, King Priam. I was planning to go there myself after breakfast to see if I could spot my husband, Hector, on the battlefield."

"You are the wife of Hector?" said Alex, just as amazed as his sister, "Then your name must be Andromache."

"Right you are, little man. You and your sister are both very intelligent. Alexander, you shall hold my hand as we climb the steps to the watchtower. And you, Anastasia, if you would like, may hold Astyanax in your arms. He's a big boy, but a very friendly one. Would you like to carry him?"

"Oh yes, ma'am," she said with a grin, "I would love to."

With that, the three of them made their way to the top of the watchtower. It was a long climb, and they were all a little bit out of breath when they arrived, but it was well worth the effort. The view from the watchtower was simply incredible. They could see for miles in every direction.

The tower was crowded with people, but all of the hustle and bustle seemed centered around a single figure sitting on a high chair. Around this figure sat a group of old men who looked even wiser than they were old. The figure in the chair was not particularly tall, but he sat up so straight in the chair and had such an air of dignity about him that he seemed ten feet tall. His hair and beard were white, but his eyes looked young; they were almost the eyes of a child. Try to picture in your mind the perfect soldier combined with the perfect grandfather. If you can do that, then you will come pretty close to imagining what the man in the chair looked like. He was, of course, King Priam.

As the children looked on, Priam turned to the old men and spoke with them quietly. They were his royal advisors, his council of elders, and they were discussing the war. For a moment, their conversation seemed to get almost heated, when, suddenly, they all stopped speaking at once and turned their heads to the right. A woman was coming toward them. She had long dark hair that fell over her shoulders in a cascade of thick curls. Her eyes were deep brown and seemed to draw into them all the light and air around her. She moved slowly and with a steady, graceful sway as if she were walking in a dream. It was impossible to look at her quickly and then turn away. Once your eyes fell upon her face, you had to study it: had to follow the curves of her eyebrows and nose and chin. It was a face that you could get lost in.

"Alas," said Priam softly, "No blame could come on any man or army that fought and died for such a woman. Her face is like the night sky when all the stars shine in unison, and men are driven wild by the sight so that they will risk all for adventure and discovery. Come closer, Helen, my child, no one here blames you. Let us look together on the battlefield. Perhaps there you shall see your rightful lord, Menelaus, and the friends you left behind in Greece."

"Dear father," she said, and her voice was like honey in its sweetness, "How I wish I had died on that day that Paris carried me away, and I brought death to you and your city. Better yet, I wish my nurse had taken me as a baby and thrown me into the sea. Every day, as the battle rages outside the walls, I weave it all into my tapestry. My needle has captured the soldiers in their glory and their tragedy. Even you, good king, have your place in the web. What more can I do? The gods have measured out our destiny, and some day we shall all be characters in a song. It is the gods, the gods who drive us to our ruin."

Alex wanted to cry out that it was not the gods but the Accuser who was causing Greek and Trojan to fall upon each other with such hatred and strife. He may have been only nine, but he was already beginning to understand. True, the Greek gods could be petty, vain, and cruel, as Hera, Athena, and Aphrodite had been when they fought for the Golden Apple; still, what was happening here at Troy pointed to an evil force much deeper than the gods. This was more than war; it was a kind of madness, a disease that devoured everything in its path. But he thought it wiser to remain silent for the time being.

"Helen," said Priam, "tell me now the names of these noble Greek warriors that I see below me. Who is this one in the front who seems a head taller than all the rest? He looks like a great shepherd leading his sheep to pasture."

"That, my father, is the great Agamemnon, brother to my one-time husband. He it is who commands all the armies of Greece in the name of Menelaus."

"And who are those two men beside him? One seems older than I while the other seems the same age as my Hector. On the first, experience and wisdom seem to hang heavy like thick armor; around the second, there is the glow of wit. The mouth of the first makes me think that he is a talker; the mouth of the second tells me he studies all things before he speaks."

"You describe them well, Lord Priam. The first is Nestor, trusted advisor to High King Agamemnon. He is too old now to fight, but he never stops reminding the young soldiers how much greater the warriors of his generation were. He is usually right in whatever advice he gives. The second is Odysseus (Oh DISS ee us), King of Ithaca, the craftiest man in the whole Greek camp. He too advises Agamemnon, but he is much more careful with his words than Nestor."

"And what of these other two soldiers who seem to stand out above all the others?"

"The taller of the two, the one built like an ox and carrying a club, is Ajax. After Achilles (a KILL ees), he is the greatest and strongest of the Greek warriors. You will never hear *him* call for help, either from men or from the gods. Beside him is Diomedes (die oh MEE dees). He, my Lord, is like Hector in his strength and his self-control. When the moment calls for cool thinking and a level head, the Greeks can always count on Diomedes. He is a man of balance."

"What a shame, daughter. Were it not for this war I would be proud to count such men among my friends. If only Paris had remained on Mount Ida and had never traveled to Greece. Ah well, there is nothing for us to do but sit here and watch the finest warriors of Greece and Troy slaughter each other on the field of battle. Every day they forget more and more their honor and their virtue. From up here, I have seen men with swords kill others who were defenseless. No longer do they take prisoners and accept ransom. It is blood they want, only blood. No, Helen, all we can do is watch and pray until this madness has run its course."

"No!" shouted Alex, "No! If you do that you will only be doing what the Accuser wants you to do."

"Who is this child who speaks so boldly?" said Priam, "He reminds me of my own Hector when he was a boy."

"Forgive me, father," said Andromache, "It is I who brought the boy and his sister. They wanted to see Helen, and they were such good children that I couldn't refuse them."

"Come over here, boy," said Priam, "and tell me what is on your mind."

"O King," said Alex, trying to sound as grown-up as he could, "You must not sit by silently while this madness continues. You must stop it. You must remind your soldiers and those of Greece of their nobility and their virtue. It is not right that heroes should forget about honor. What will the men of the future think when they look back to the Trojan War and see only hatred and strife?"

"Yes, yes," said Stacey, running over to Alex and taking his hand, "If there are two boys and they both want the same girl, then let them fight for her. Why must both armies fight? In all the stories I know, if a boy steals a girl away from the man she loves, then the boy and the man fight a duel and the winner gets the girl. That is the honorable thing to do, isn't it?"

"Of course, my girl," said Priam, "of course. Perhaps it could work."

Priam rose from his chair and began calling out orders. For the next hour or so, there was much shouting and running to and fro, and the children could see much activity on the battlefield. In the end, the armies of Greece and Troy lined up in two rows facing each other across an empty space. Into that space, dressed in full armor and carrying spears, Paris and Menelaus stepped forth. It was going to happen! The two soldiers would fight a single duel, and the winner would take Helen. Whoever won, the war would end, and the Greeks would go home.

"Ha!" shouted Alex, looking up into the air, "What do you think about that, you old Accuser? The soldiers won't listen to you anymore. They will do the right thing instead."

The duel was both an exciting and a terrible thing to watch. After they had circled each other three times like lions circling their prey, Paris raised his spear and hurled it with all his might at Menelaus. The spear hit his shield directly in the middle and tore its way through the first eight layers. But the ninth layer, made of thick leather from the hide of a mountain goat, held fast and stopped the spear. Menelaus pulled out the spear and tossed it on the ground. Then, with a mighty war cry, he hurled his own spear at Paris's head.

The spear flew straight and true, but Paris moved quickly to the right. It missed his head and instead struck his armor where the shoulder comes close to the neck. The armor fell away, exposing the left side of his neck and chest. Paris was not injured, but the force of the spear knocked him to his feet.

When Menelaus saw Paris fall, he pulled his sword out from the sheath at his side and charged. Holding the hilt of the blade with two hands, he brought it crashing down on Paris' exposed neck. But before the sword could strike him, Paris rolled out from under it and sprang to his feet. He too pulled out his sword and made a rush at Menelaus.

Again and again, their swords clanged against each other so that the air around them vibrated with the sound. Alex could almost swear that the tower itself shook with each blow. For awhile, Paris held his own, but it soon became clear that Menelaus was the stronger warrior. With a tremendous blow that could have cut a tree trunk in half, Menelaus swung his sword at Paris. Sword met sword, and Paris was sent flying to the ground. As the fallen warrior lay on his back, Menelaus strode toward him like a giant. Each of his steps made the earth beneath him rumble. This time, Paris would not roll out from under his blade. With the force of a tornado, Menelaus brought his blade down again on the exposed neck of his enemy.

And now, surely, Paris would have been killed and Helen returned to her rightful lord. But the Accuser would not give up that easily. He flew quickly to the side of Aphrodite and whispered in her ear that Menelaus was about to get the better of her and kill Paris whom she loved and who had given her the Golden Apple. (By now, Alex and Stacey had guessed something that even Daddy did not know: that Eris, the goddess of strife who had made the Golden Apple, was really the Accuser in disguise.) Faster than the name

Aphrodite could flow in and out of your mind, the goddess of love flew to the side of Paris and covered him in a thick cloud. Then, as Menelaus howled in rage at the trick, she lifted Paris up in her arms and carried him to the bed of Helen. Then, Aphrodite drew away Helen as well and brought her, angry and all unwilling, to Paris.

Those on the tower opened their eyes and mouths in wonder as they saw Helen disappear from their midst. But they were quickly distracted by a terrible scream from the battlefield. The Accuser, not content merely to spoil the duel, had whispered more of his poison into the ear of a Trojan:

"You can't trust these Greeks. They will kill your wives and children and burn your homes to the ground. You can't beat them by playing by the rules. They care nothing for honor or virtue. Now, do as I tell you. Take up your bow and shoot one of your arrows at Menelaus. If you kill him in this manner, all Troy will sing your praises."

"No," said the Trojan, "I have never shot a man like that. It would dishonor me and my family and all of Troy."

"Don't speak like a child," answered the Accuser, "This is not a game where you must shake your opponent's hand before you begin. This is war. All is permitted as long as it helps you to defeat your enemy. Menelaus would do the same if he were in your position."

"Yes, you are right, he would do the same." Actually, to tell the truth, the Trojan did not really believe that Menelaus would do the same thing, but the Accuser had so corrupted his mind that he was ready to call black white and white black if only it might bring him the glory of a kill. And so, pulling an arrow from his quiver, he notched it to the string and sent it soaring. The arrow whistled in the wind and struck Menelaus in the thigh where there was a break in his armor. Dark red blood flowed freely on to the grass, and Menelaus let out a cry:

"My fellow Greeks, we are betrayed. Let us fall upon these Trojan dogs!"

And with that, the two armies fell upon each other like vultures that fall on the dead bodies of animals and tear them to pieces with their hooked talons and their sharp beaks. A cloud of dust rose up from the battlefield, and soon, those on the tower could not tell which soldier was Trojan and which was Greek.

"Oh!" said Stacey with horror, and covered her eyes with her hands. But Alex continued to look, and the more he looked the more angry he got. The Accuser had beaten him. There was no doubt about that. He walked right over to the edge of the tower and looked down on the battle, hoping that an idea would come to him. He tried to focus his thoughts, and he stared as intently as an eagle in search of its prey. And because he was staring so intently, he saw something that no one else on the tower saw.

A single Trojan soldier had broken away from the battle and was running toward the wall. He was the most handsome and well-built man that Alex had ever seen. There was great purpose in his eyes. This man was not running away because he was afraid but because he had some mission to fulfill. Alex knew at once who he was. He was Hector, son of Priam, husband of Andromache, the leader and guide of the army of Troy.

In a loud voice, Hector cried out: "Open the Scaean (SKEE an) Gates! I must enter."

"C'mon, Stacey," said Alex, grabbing his sister by the hand, "We need to go back down to the palace. We must speak with Hector."

The people on the tower were so hypnotized by the battle that they did not even notice when Alex and Stacey, hand in hand, slipped away and ran down the stairs.

The Noble Enemy

As they both had good memories, Alex and Stacey had no trouble finding their way back to the palace. When they arrived, they found things far less peaceful than they had been that morning. People were running around now in a wild panic, and there was worry written on the faces of all the men and women who passed by them.

Eventually, they found themselves in the main hall of the palace. At its center was a great hearthstone with a fire burning on it. And on the stone, there stood a woman whom Stacey wanted to call Eve. She seemed the mother of a whole race or tribe. If Andromache looked like she *could* have ten children, then this woman looked like she had had that many children—that many and more. Her eyes, like those of Andromache, also had the look of one who watches, but the lines and circles in her face were much deeper, deep as wounds. Andromache laughed so she would not cry, but this woman looked as if she had cried a river through her tired eyes and still had an ocean of tears hidden within. She was Hecuba, wife of Priam and the queen of all Troy.

Alex approached as if he would speak to her, but as he did, the door to the hall burst open, and Hector came running in, his hands and his armor dripping with blood.

"My son!" cried Hecuba, "Praise be to Zeus that you have returned to me. Come, we shall sacrifice together to the gods."

"No mother, no," said Hector gently but firmly, "I am covered with the blood of men. I dare not come before the gods like this. But you, mother, you must go to the tower and offer prayers to the goddess Athena. Perhaps she will hear you and forgive our city for the recklessness of my brother. Meanwhile, I shall go to Paris myself and drag him, if I must, back into the battle. It is for him that we are fighting, yet he stays in here by the side of his wife. And then, when I have done that, I shall bid farewell to my own wife, Andromache, and my son, Astyanax. The battle has grown fierce, mother, and I fear that I may not return again to Troy."

"My son, you are tired and sore. Come have a glass of wine with me, and we shall talk together of the battle."

"No, mother, please do not tempt me to do such a thing. My men yearn for my return, and I must not cloud my thinking with wine. The spirit within me urges me back to the field of battle, where men win glory. I must not delay a moment."

Hecuba opened her lips as if she would speak again but instead let out a long sigh. She knew she could not hold him back. It was his lot to fight just as it was hers to suffer in silence.

Hector bent over and kissed his mother on each cheek, careful not to smear her dress with blood. Then he turned and ran to the chamber of Helen and Paris. Alex and Stacey followed him and stood in the shadow of the chamber door.

Helen sat at the loom weaving her tapestry, while Paris sat beside her polishing his armor. When Hector entered the room, Helen stood up and ran to him, but Paris did not move or speak.

"Brother," she said, "I hope you have come to take Paris with you. How I wish I had been carried away by a better man. This Paris has no shame, but sits here in his chamber while his men fight for him."

"Dear sister," said Hector, "I do not blame you for what has happened. But this Paris, who can understand him? One minute he is hot; the next minute he is cold. One day he will fight at the front of his troops; the next day he will cower in the back like a scared child. Truly he is without shame."

Hector smiled kindly on Helen and touched her shoulder with his hand. Then, he turned toward Paris and spoke to him harshly: "Brother, what would become of our city if all men were like you? Without our sense of shame that drives us to seek virtue and turn from evil we would all be lost. Our world would fall into chaos, and the strong would drive the weak into the dust.

"You know the code as well as I, Paris. We who are the warriors, whether we be Greek or Trojan, are given the best of everything: the most fertile land, the choicest meats, the most beautiful women. They are our prizes, our meeds of honor. But to win them, we must fight and live with honor. It is our lot to amass such prizes that our glory might live forever and that others will speak of us with praise after we are in our graves. Truly, brother, if we were like the gods and could live forever, then I would not tell you to fight. But since our lives are short and the need to win glory presses on us so heavily, then *let* us fight that we might win that glory.

"Once already you violated the code, Paris, when you stole away Menelaus' greatest prize. Your act was a shameful one, carried out by deceit and cunning. And now you have allowed yourself to be shamefully rescued from the fighting and have robbed Menelaus of his chance to reclaim his wife. Think, Paris, think! Your actions can only lead to disaster."

"Hector, my brother, always you scold me rightly, never too severely, but in keeping with what is just and proper. Even as you spoke, I felt the blood rush into my heart and a new longing for honorable battle impel me to fight in the foremost ranks of the Trojans. Return, Hector, to the battlefield, for your men need you. I shall put my armor back on and meet you at the Gates."

"See to it, brother, that you keep to your word."

Then, without waiting for Paris to reply, Hector ran out of Helen's chamber and headed for his own, the very one where Alex and Stacey had had breakfast that morning. Three times he circled the chamber, three times he called out Andromache's name, but his wife was nowhere to be found.

"Please, sir," said Alex, stepping into Hector's chamber, "If you are looking for your wife, we know where she is. Please, follow us, and we will lead you to her."

Hector, who was too anxious and excited to ask the children why they—strangers whom he had never met—should know the whereabouts of his wife, followed Alex and Stacey as they ran back to the tower and began to climb the stairs. They expected, for the second time that day, to follow the stairs to the very top, but, lo and behold, as they reached the half-way point and stopped on a landing to catch their breath, Andromache came running down to them from above.

And it was there, half-way up, between earth and sky, between the battlefield below and the tower above, that Hector and his beloved Andromache met and shared their final embrace. The meeting did not last very long, but to Alex and Stacey, it seemed to last forever: a moment frozen in time that could never age or decay.

Andromache, who was carrying Astyanax, walked over to Stacey and placed the baby in her arms. Then, like a waterfall rushing down a mountain, she fell into the waiting arms of Hector. Crying as she smiled—or was it laughing through her tears; the children could never decide—Andromache looked up into her husband's eyes and spoke:

"My dear husband, what a strange and wonderful man you are. Even as you stand here beside me, I can see that your eyes look over me to the battlefield. Hector, it is your own great strength that will destroy you, even as Helen's beauty has led to her ruin and that of her family. I know how greatly you love me and our child, and yet still you long to be back fighting with your men. Hector, it is I who need you more. To me you are not only husband, but father and brother as well. All who once belonged to me are dead, killed by the dreadful Achilles. You and Astyanax are all that I have left. What shall I do if you too should fall beneath the spear of Achilles or some other among the Greek camp?"

"Andromache, dear one, all these things you say are true. But my spirit will not let me remain here within the walls. I have learned it all to well: to fight always with courage in the foremost ranks; to win glory for my father and my city; to honor the gods and give them a portion of the prizes I win."

When Hector spoke these words, Alex straightened up his back and took a deep breath. They reminded him of a pledge that a Boy Scout might recite from memory. Perhaps Daddy and Pan were right after all. Perhaps the virtues of these soldiers of old really *were* the foundation of all that was best and most noble in our civilization. Surely this was the way to fight the Accuser. Yes, Hector would have to return to the battle, Alex could see that now, and, yes, in that battle he might lose his life, but if he stayed true to his code and the virtues on which it rested, all would be well.

"Andromache," said Hector, as if he had just read Alex's thoughts, "we are not free to live any way that we like. We each have our lot in life and our duty to perform. Long ago, Zeus decided the day of my death. Why should I try to escape it? Let me rather seek to complete the task that has been given me. I must return to my soldiers; without me, they are lost.

"But you, Andromache, you must leave this watchtower and return to your chamber. Even now, Helen works at her loom weaving her tapestry. You too, dear one, must attend to the loom. If peace should ever return to our fair city, we will have need of beautiful clothes and of rugs and tapestries to adorn our floors and walls. Go now, Andromache, but first, where is my son that I may hold him one last time?"

Stacey, who had been listening, almost in a trance, to every word that Hector spoke, lifted up the child and handed him to his father. Stacey expected that the child would giggle and laugh when he saw him, but instead, the child let out a scream of fright.

"Of course," said Stacey in a loud voice, "It's your helmet, Hector, your helmet that is frightening the baby."

Stacey was right. Hector had been in such a hurry that he had forgotten to remove his helmet from his head. It was a massive helmet, made of bronze and padded with leather. Along the top from back to front there ran a crest of dark horsehair that shivered and nodded in the breeze. Astyanax had good reason to be afraid of it!

Hector placed the baby back in Stacey's arms and removed his helmet. The baby stopped crying at once, and Hector took him up again and tossed him high in the air. Then, throwing back his head and lifting up his chest, the great Hector laughed. Neither Alex nor Stacey had ever heard such a laugh. It was as deep and majestic as the mountains and as joyful and free as the song of a hundred skylarks soaring toward the morning sun. It was a laugh that the Accuser could never defeat, a laugh that he could not even understand.

Hector reached out and drew Andromache to him. For one last, long moment, father, mother, and child shared in a loving embrace.

"O Zeus," cried out Hector, "Grant that my son shall be a greater man than his father. May he make glad the heart of his mother and be spoken of with praise at the Scaean Gates."

And then, it was over. Hector was running back down the stairs, his heart eager for the fighting and the company of his men. As he neared the Gates, Paris, dressed in full armor and with the setting sun shining off his bronze helmet, ran to his side. Together, they charged out to the battlefield like wild stallions who have broken out of their corral and who gallop wildly toward the hills on which they were born.

"Alex," said Stacey, after Andromache had led them back to the courtyard and returned to her chamber, "I just don't get it. I thought the Greeks were supposed to be the good guys and the Trojans the bad guys. But everyone we've met so far seems very nice. I don't think I've ever met anyone as brave and as strong and as kind as Hector. I could live in this city for years and years. Who is the enemy, Alex?"

"Well, Stacey," he said, after thinking for a moment, "If Hector is the enemy, then he is the most noble enemy I've ever met. No, the enemy is not Greece or Troy. It is the Accuser. Maybe that's why Pan led us here first, so that we would understand that Troy is not the evil one. I mean, think about it, Stacey: if one man or one city or one country was evil, then we could just destroy it and everything would be good from then on. At least that's what I used to think. But now I'm starting to wonder. Perhaps the evil doesn't lie in a single enemy, but in each one of us—in all those terrible things that we do when we listen to the words of the Accuser. I'll bet that Trojan who shot Menelaus with the arrow was as good a man as anyone we met today in Troy, and yet look what terror he caused by listening to the Accuser."

"Oh, Alex," said Stacey, with a look of pride on her face, "I didn't understand everything you said, but I just know that Daddy would tell you that he was proud of you if he were here. But, Alex, I'm afraid. Something inside me tells me that it is time we leave this city and go out to the Greek camp."

"Yes, Stacey, I agree with you, though I can't say that I like the idea of going out there. In about thirty minutes it will be dark. Maybe if we walk over to the Gates, we can find a way to get outside."

"Yes, Alex," said Stacey, taking his hand and giving it a squeeze, "Let's go now, before we change our mind."

As the sun set behind them, the children slowly made their way to the Scaean Gates. In order to keep their courage firm, they stared straight ahead and did not look back even once. And it was for that reason that neither one of them noticed that a woman dressed in a dark cloak had been following them for the last ten minutes.

— Chapter —

9

Riddles in the Dark

"A lex," said Stacey, when they had almost reached the Gates, "did you just hear something strange?"

"Yes, Stacey, it sounded like someone mumbling or maybe chanting."

"Apollo... Apollo... speak... no... pain... strife... AYYYYYY!"

"Run, Stacey!" yelled Alex, but they couldn't run for the wall was directly in front of them. Not knowing what else to do, they spun around and started to run back in the direction of the palace. They never made it. Before they could run even twenty feet, they found themselves face-to-face with the dark figure of a woman. Her arms were raised up in the air, and she held a golden staff in her right hand. There was a crown of garlands around her head and more garlands hanging from her neck. In a fit of panic, Alex and Stacey tried to run to the left, but the woman was too fast for them. Like the wings of a hawk, her two arms swooped down and caught the children in a tight embrace.

"Help!" screamed Stacey, as she tried to bite the woman's arm. But again she was too fast for them. With one swift motion, she wrapped her cloak around the children's heads. Then, with soothing words, like the words one hears in a dream, she spoke:

"Do not be afraid, children, you are safe. I have not come to harm you but to warn you. I am Cassandra, daughter of Priam and priestess of Apollo. The god blessed me with the gift of prophecy, but with that gift there came a dreadful curse. Though my vision is clear and I speak the truth about the things that are to come, no one believes me until it is too late. To them, my words are riddles, dark sayings that they cannot understand. But you children are from the future (yes, I can see that with my second sight) and so perhaps you can hear and understand. Listen then and be warned of the dangers that lie before you.

"This morning you heard Helen speak the name of swift-footed Achilles, the greatest warrior who ever fought with sword and spear. But you may have noticed that Achilles was missing from the field of battle. No one in the city of Troy, not even Helen, knows the reason for Achilles' absence. But the god Apollo has revealed it to me and so shall I reveal it to you.

"Many weeks ago, during a lull in the fighting, the Greeks mounted a raid on the nearby city of Thebe. With Achilles in the lead, they sacked the city and took all its treasure for their spoils.

Among those spoils were two women, lovely in form and in face. Of the two, the most beautiful and noble was Chryseis (KRIS ee iss). By rights, she should have gone to Achilles as his prize, but Agamemnon, by power of his command, took her for himself. The second of the two, Briseis (BRIS ee is), he gave to Achilles, not with honor and gratitude, but grudgingly.

"Several days later, as the Kings of Greece feasted on the meat they had taken from Thebe, a lone man, lost and defenseless, stumbled into their camp. His name was Chryses (CRY sees), and he had come to the Greeks, humbled and afraid, in order to beg Agamemnon to return to him his one and only child: Chryseis. In exchange for his daughter, he offered Agamemnon noble ransom, but Agamemnon refused. And this, children, was a fault in him.

"Though you did not know it, I was by your side when you overheard Hector speaking to Paris about the code of honor by which the soldiers live. Of them it is expected that they shall heed the prayers of the weak—of the guest, of the suppliant, of the stranger in the land—and show hospitality to all. The ransom that Chryses offered was a fair one, and Agamemnon was honor-bound to accept it. But he would not. Rather, he treated the old man with contempt and even threatened to kill him if he should ever return to the Greek camp.

"Afraid for his life, Chryses departed quickly, but he would have his revenge. Even as I am, Chryses is a servant of the god Apollo, and as he walked home through the night, he called down a terrible curse on the heads of Agamemnon and all the Greeks. Apollo was swift to hear and swift to act. From the top of Mount Olympus he leapt down, and the arrows in his golden quiver rattled fiercely on his back. From that quiver, he drew a single black arrow and shot it into the center of the Greek camp. With it came the creeping death that stalks in the night: disease, death, plague. One by one, the soldiers of Greece fell ill and died. All their prayers and their medicines were useless against the plague. For nine days, disease spread throughout the camp, till the air was thick with the cries of pain and the smoke that rose from the funeral pyres. And throughout those terrible days, where was Agamemnon: hiding in his tent like a coward.

"On the tenth day, the noble heart of Achilles could stand it no longer. Seizing the right that normally belonged to Agamemnon alone, he called for a meeting of all the Kings of Greece and brought to it a priest with the power of prophecy: Calchas (KAL kus). Achilles commanded Calchas to speak before all the kings and reveal the cause of the plague. Calchas was nervous, afraid that his words would anger a man of great power, but Achilles swore that he would protect Calchas from all harm. And so Calchas spoke. His words were few and to the point: the plague would not be lifted until Agamemnon returned Chryseis to her father without accepting any ransom in return.

"Oh, Agamemnon's fury was great! 'What,' he cried, 'Shall I be the only soldier who must go without a prize?' But, of course, as commander of his men, Agamemnon knew he would have to return her. Second by second, his fury was cooling down. But another few minutes and he would have given the girl back peacefully."

"And then, foolishly, stubbornly, madly, Achilles rose to his feet. The Accuser had whispered in his ear (yes, children, I too know of the Accuser) that this was his chance to humiliate Agamemnon before the Greeks and get his revenge. 'O proud Agamemnon,' he cried, 'most greedy and grasping of men, there are no prizes left to give you. It is better that you should go without a prize than that you should seek another from your men. Fight well in battle tomorrow, and perhaps you shall win another prize.'

"A hushed silence fell over the council until, eager to cause more strife, the Accuser moved into the ear of Agamemnon and roused him to fury as well. 'You cannot let Achilles threaten you like that,' he whispered, 'If the men see you give in to him, they will never follow you again. Already the men prefer Achilles to you. They all know that Achilles is the strongest and deserves the most prizes.'

"That was all Agamemnon needed to hear. The blood rushed into his face, and he lashed back at Achilles with his own threat. 'Very well, Achilles, I shall return Chryseis to her father, but in exchange I shall take Briseis away from you. I am the commander-in-chief, and it would be wrong that I should be left naked and without a prize.'

"Back and forth the heroes quarreled. All the anger and hatred and frustration that had been building up for nine years spilled out and swept them away. In the end, Achilles' wrath grew so great that he drew his sword from his side and prepared to kill Agamemnon. But Mount Olympus was watching. Hera spoke to Athena and sent her flying to the side of Achilles. Invisible to all but Achilles, Athena grabbed him by the hair and pulled him back. She spoke directly to his heart and told him to spare the life of Agamemnon. Achilles obeyed, but from that very hour he refused to fight any more on the side of the Greeks. If his own prize could be taken from him that easily, why should he risk his life any further? Hadn't the war itself begun when Paris stole Helen away from her rightful lord? Was Achilles' love for Briseis any less than Menelaus' for Helen? No, he thought, it was better that he pull out now and leave Agamemnon to fight his own battles.

"And so, along with all his men, Achilles returned to his tent. He was the greatest and strongest of all the warriors, but he was also young and impulsive and given to outbursts of anger. Though his father was a mortal man, his mother was a goddess who dwelt in the sea. Her name was Thetis (THEE tis), and though she loved Achilles dearly, she was tormented day and night by the knowledge that he would die young. Throughout his childhood, she would warn him again and again that his life would be short and that he would never live to see old age. Hearing such things for so many years had caused the young warrior to become obsessed with death and to vow to himself that if it were indeed his destiny to die young, he would meet that death having amassed more glory than any man before or after him.

"Troubled and confused now by the actions of Agamemnon, Achilles no sooner reached his tent than he cried out to his mother for help. As swift as a wave that crashes on the shore, Thetis came and sat by his side. Achilles told her all that had happened and begged her to fly to Zeus and seek his help. 'Mother,' he said, 'Tell Zeus that if he loves and honors you that he must cause the Greeks to start losing this war. Let him fill the Trojans with courage and strength that they might defeat the Greeks. So let them perish one by one until Agamemnon comes himself to my tent and begs me to return to the war. Then shall the Greeks know what fools they were to insult the best of their warriors. Then shall they give me gifts and prizes in keeping with my worth.'

"It was a terrible prayer, one that even the Accuser would be hard pressed to devise, but Thetis carried it to Zeus, and Zeus granted it with a nod of his divine head. Even now, children, the prayer of Achilles is beginning to bear its evil fruit. Hector and Paris have gone together to the battlefield, and soon they will begin to defeat their enemy. Soon the blood of a hundred Greek warriors will lie spilled on the earth. If this continues, Hector will soon kill one whom Achilles loves dearly, and Achilles, in revenge, will kill Hector. And if Hector dies, then all Troy will die with him.

"But go now children. I will show you where there is a hidden break in the wall known only to Priam. Through that passage you must slip out of Troy while most of the guards are asleep. Seek out the tent of Achilles. Speak to him. Convince him, if you can, to return to the war. Perhaps you can turn aside the tragedy that is to come. You are our only hope."

Cassandra took their hands and led them swiftly to the secret passage. Before they knew it, they were outside the wall, and Cassandra had disappeared into the night.

"Are you ready, Alex?" said Stacey.

"Yes, Stacey, I am."

And with that, the two children, tired, scared, and alone, made their way into the Greek camp.

— Part —
2

The Wrath of Achilles

"*Upon the earth*
Two Strifes exist; the one is praised by those
Who come to know her, and the other blamed.
Their natures differ: for the cruel one
Makes battle thrive, and war."
—Hesiod

— Chapter —

10

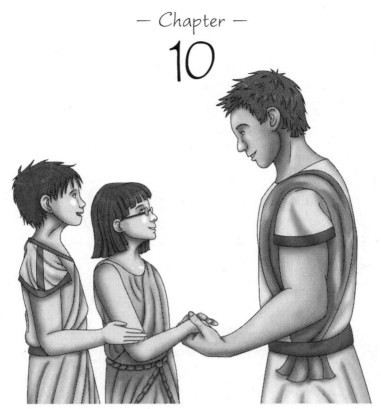

In the Tent of Achilles

There is one story about Achilles that everyone knows. It is not mentioned anywhere in the two epics of Homer, and yet, still, everyone knows it. It is the story of Achilles' birth, and of how, when the infant was less than a day old, his goddess mother carried him down into the shadowy realms of Hades. Through those realms of perpetual night, there runs a stream whose water is as black as pitch and whose smell is like that of burning sulfur. Its name is the river Styx, and if ever a god, even Zeus himself, should swear by it, he can never break his oath.

Into those terrible waters, Thetis dipped her son, for she knew that by doing so, she would render his skin impervious to all weapons. But, alas, in her haste to finish the deed and return to the land of the living, she made a fatal error. When she had dipped the child, she had held him by his heel, and, as a result, that heel had never known the touch of stygian waters. That mistake would someday return to haunt the great warrior. For you see, although neither sword nor spear nor arrow could penetrate Achilles' body, the slightest scratch could break through the skin of his heel. In the end, the legends tell us, Achilles was slain by Paris who, aided by Apollo, shot a poisoned arrow into his heel. Today we still use the phrase "Achilles' heel" to mean a weak spot or a moral flaw in an otherwise noble person.

It is a wonderful story and one worth retelling, but I would encourage you to put it aside for now. The Achilles whom Alex and Stacey would soon meet was a great warrior indeed, but his greatness did not rest on some trick of his birth. It was not magic waters but his own brave heart that made Achilles the hero that he was. If his skill in battle surpassed that of all others, it was only because he spent every waking moment training his body for the fight. For Achilles, there was nothing else. The battlefield was his world, and on it he reigned supreme.

And yet, now, for the first time in his life, Achilles was on the outside looking in. While the fighting raged around him, he sat idle in his tent. Fingers that yearned to close themselves around the hilt of a bronze sword now lay open and empty. Armor that was the terror of his enemies now hung useless on the wall.

When Alex and Stacey, drawn by the same destiny that had brought them back in time, arrived in the tent of Achilles, they did not find him exercising his muscles or sharpening his spear or cleaning the blood from his sword. Rather they found him sitting on the floor of his tent gently strumming a lyre. And as he strummed, he sang:

> Life is brief, but fame is long;
> Soldier's glories live in song.
> On the field their bodies lie,
> But their mem'ries never die.
>
> Shining in the sun they fight;
> Huge and splendid in their might.
> Never flinching from the knife;
> Wreathed in glory all their life.
>
> With their sword and spear they win
> Gold and copper, bronze and tin;
> Weapons, armor, horses swift,
> Such they merit as their gift.
>
> Future ages shall recall
> They, for honor, gave their all.
> Life is brief, but fame is long;
> May their glories live in song.

Beside Achilles, listening to his song in silence, sat a young man whose face seemed too kind and gentle to be that of a soldier. As the warrior finished his song, the young man stood and began to pace back and forth across the floor of the tent.

"Please, Patroclus (pa TROW klus), my friend, sit down. Be at peace."

"No, Achilles, no. You *must* return to the battle. The Greeks yearn for your return. Without you, they fear the sword of Hector. Do not punish them for the evil of Agamemnon. And what of your own men? Did we make the long sea journey from Greece just to sit idle in our tents? If you cannot forgive Agamemnon, then at least have pity on your own men, Achilles. They, too, long to win glory for themselves."

"All that you say moves my heart, Patroclus, but I cannot forget the injury that Agamemnon has done to my honor. He has treated me as if I were a beggar or a slave. Always I fight the hardest in the battle; always I return exhausted, torn, and bloodied. Yet always the greatest prizes go to him, and I am left to slink off to my tent with some small thing. Never does he praise me before the men for my courage. I am ignored."

"But Achilles, all the Kings of Greece sing your praises."

"Yes, but Agamemnon remains silent. From him I receive only scorn. Oh, ye gods that dwell on Mount Olympus, when shall you hear my cries and vindicate me?"

"They have heard, Achilles," said a voice from outside the tent, "We have come."

"Who speaks?" said Achilles, rising and walking toward the entrance, "Enter, strangers. Here you shall find welcome."

With weak knees and fluttering stomachs, Alex and Stacey entered the tent. Alex never knew what had impelled him to speak those words, but they seemed to have worked. Though Achilles paused for a moment when he saw the two children, he soon reached out his hands and drew them in. His hands felt rough, like sandpaper, and his grip was very tight.

"Do the gods send us children, Patroclus? Truly their ways are beyond knowing. Still, let us show our guests the hospitality due all strangers. Who knows? Perhaps they are Apollo and his sister, Artemis, in disguise. Come, children, and dine with us. Our table is your table."

"My name, Achilles, is Alex and my sister's name is Stacey. We thank you for your hospitality and are honored to share your meal. We have come a long way to meet with you."

The children sat down at the table with Achilles and Patroclus and feasted with them in grand style. Achilles may have been terrible on the battlefield and stubborn about his honor, but as a host, he was second to none. But when the four of them had satisfied their hunger and the desire for food had gone from their mind and body, Alex stood up and, pushing his chair away from him, he spoke strong words to the swift-footed warrior:

"Achilles, we thank you again for your hospitality, but I am afraid that we must add our own words to those of Patroclus. You *must* return to the battle. If you do not, great evil will result. I wish that this war had never happened, but just yesterday Stacey and I learned from a warrior as great and noble as yourself that glory and honor are still possible, even in a war that should not have been fought. You are a soldier, Achilles; it is your gift and your calling. When you are not fighting, you are not yourself. You must do your duty and fulfill your destiny."

"You speak wisely, young man," said Achilles, "but still I cannot forgive the harsh words spoken by Agamemnon before all the Kings of Greece. And there is another reason, but I cannot tell it to you now. It is in my mind, but I cannot find the words to express it. New ideas are racing through my brain. I am beginning to wonder if …"

Before Achilles could finish his sentence, a great cry of pain rose up in the still morning air. Achilles, Patroclus, and the children ran to the entrance and flung it open. They were greeted by a chaos of dust and screams.

"Quick children," said Achilles, "run to the battlefield and find out what is happening. I have sworn not to leave my tent, and I will stick to my oath. But you two are free to observe. Go and see, and then return to me with whatever news you can gather."

It did not even cross Alex and Stacey's mind that they might disobey or question Achilles' command. Five seconds later, they were out of the tent and running full speed toward the battlefield.

— Chapter —

11

The Embassy

It did not take Alex and Stacey long to realize that things were not going well for the Greek army. The tide of battle had turned, and the Greeks had lost their edge. A new strength and ferocity had filled the hearts of the Trojans, and they pressed against their enemy with the force of a tornado rushing over a cornfield.

Perhaps you have seen the same thing happen in a basketball game. The visiting team has the upper hand and begins to make baskets with amazing speed. For a while, they seem unstoppable. Then, the coach of the home team calls a timeout and groups his players into a huddle. With all the energy and enthusiasm he can muster, he challenges his players to remember their skill and regain their focus, and suddenly, almost magically, they find their nerve again. In a word, they get back their psych. Like lightning, a new sense of confidence draws them together into a team, and they rush back onto the court with a renewed desire to win at all costs. The thrill of it is electric, and it has the double effect of raising the courage of the home team while draining it away from their opponents.

Something like that was happening now on the grassy playing field that stretched out before the Walls of Troy. Hector, the Trojan's "coach," had rallied his men with a stirring speech, and had lit a fire of courage in each of their hearts. As Alex and Stacey watched with horror, one Greek soldier after the other was run to ground like a helpless fox before a determined hunting party. By sunset, the army was in shambles, and many of the best warriors were left dead or injured. As the men hobbled back to their barracks to dress their wounds and get some much needed rest, the Kings of Greece gathered in Agamemnon's tent for an emergency meeting. The children followed and hid themselves just outside the doorway.

Diomedes spoke first: "Lord Agamemnon, once before you scolded me when you saw me hanging back from battle. At that time, I accepted your rebuke in silence and roused myself to action. So now, Agamemnon, I return your rebuke. If you do not act soon, our army will be lost. You must do what you can to lure Achilles back into the battle. Without him, I fear we shall not last another day. These Trojans fight with the fury of the god of war."

"You speak rightly, Diomedes," replied Agamemnon, "Oh what folly was mine when I dared to insult the finest warrior of Greece."

"I warned you, Agamemnon," said Nestor, "that your rashness would be your undoing. But let us not dwell on that now. There is still a way that this situation can be resolved, but it will cost you dearly, Agamemnon. You must this very night send an embassy to Achilles with an offer of ransom that he cannot refuse. You must give him much gold and fine weapons and must promise him land in Greece when he returns. And with this ransom, you must give back Briseis as well. Let him see that if he accepts your offer and takes up his sword that his honor will surpass that of all other warriors."

"Yes, wise Nestor, I shall do exactly as you suggest. But who shall I send to carry out this embassy."

"Let me see. Three men I think. The first must be Odysseus; he is wise in speech and has a persuasive tongue. The second must be Ajax; he is strong and devoted to battle and will rouse in Achilles his martial spirit. Third, you must send someone who is close to Achilles. Let it be Phoenix (FEE nix), Achilles' tutor, who is here with us in the camp and who can remind his former pupil of the code of honor in which he was raised."

"Very well," said Agamemnon, "let it be done even as you say. I shall offer the ransom you suggest and more besides."

Necessity compelled the Greeks to be swift, and within the hour, Odysseus, Ajax, and Phoenix were making their way through the night to the tent of Achilles. As for Alex and Stacey, they ran ahead to prepare Achilles for the coming embassy. Patroclus rejoiced at the news and prayed that the next morning would bring him the chance to win glory. His prayer would be answered, but not in the way he had hoped.

Ever the perfect host, Achilles welcomed the embassy into his tent, and, before any of them could speak a single word, he feasted them lavishly on meat and bread and wine. When the meal was ended, Odysseus was the first to rise and speak:

"Swift-footed Achilles, we come to you with great news! Agamemnon has relented from his former anger and has recognized your honor and worth. He asks now that you return to battle and offers you untold prizes: gold and weapons and land, and with them, Briseis herself. The army is in need of your strength and the power of your right arm. Come, the prizes and the glory await you. Take my hand in yours; it is the hand of Agamemnon extended in friendship."

"Hooray," thought Alex and Stacey to themselves, "Now Achilles will put aside his anger and return to the battlefield. Now he will see that Agamemnon honors him above all the others and that his glory and his reputation are secure. This wasn't so difficult after all."

So they thought, but it was not to be. After pondering things silently in his heart, Achilles rose and addressed the embassy:

"No, my friends, no. Do not ask me to return to the fighting. My heart is sick of battle and the ways of war. You speak of honor and glory, but I have thought long on these things, and I see that they are not as I once thought they were. Honor is the same for the brave man and the one who hangs back. We are held in a single honor by the will of Zeus: the honor that comes from being alive and from feeling the blood that flows in our veins. You list for me the prizes that Agamemnon will give me, but I tell you now that all the prizes won by the heroes of old are not worth the price of my life."

To Alex and Stacey, Achilles' words, jumbled and unsure as they were, were words that they could understand. Of course no price tag could be placed on a human life. Of course we all have value in the very fact that we are alive. They had learned as much in their second grade Sunday School class. But the impact of those words was quite different on the soldiers who heard them. Across each of their faces, a look of shock, confusion, and even horror slowly spread. To them, raised as they had been in the way of the soldier,

Achilles' words were inconceivable, unthinkable. Worse than that, they were dangerous. Let it be known in Greece and Troy that the honor of the warrior was the same as that of the shepherd or the farmer, and the whole structure of society would collapse.

"What are you saying?" said Phoenix, "have you forgotten all that I taught you? Have you cast aside the code of your father and your father's father? Before today, Achilles, none of us blamed you for staying out of the war. Oh yes, Greeks were dying because you would not fight, but still we assigned no blame. Had our prizes been stolen away, we would have done the same as you. But now that Agamemnon is laying great wealth at your feet and promising further gifts to come: now, Achilles, if you do not return, great blame will be yours. So it was in days past. The heroes of old would accept ransom, though their heart was sore, and save those who had done them wrong. The gods themselves accept offerings from those who have scorned them, and a man will forgive the murderer of his brother if the proper blood price is paid. Even so you, Achilles, must take what is offered."

"Phoenix," replied Achilles, "to me you are closer than a father, and so I will lay before you all that is on my mind. The gods have ordained it that each of us must die and pass into the realm of Hades. Until that day when Agamemnon stole my gift and I withdrew from the battlefield where men win glory, I had thought as all of you think. We must all die, so let us gain as much honor as we can before that day arrives. But a new thought appeared in my mind as I sat alone in my tent and pondered the ancient tales of heroes. I feel now in my heart that if all men must die, then we should not seek to hasten that day but that we should live.

"My mother told me once that two destinies hang over me: either I shall have a long, dull life or a short and glorious one. Until today, I had always felt that my lot was to die young in a blaze of glory, but now I wonder if the first option is not the better one. Therefore, Phoenix, when the sun rises tomorrow, I shall sail back to Greece, taking with me all of my men. You are welcome to join us in the ship, Phoenix. Return with me to Greece, and let us grow old together."

Once again, the reaction on the faces of all the soldiers was one of shock and disbelief. Achilles might as well have been speaking in a foreign language. His words and the thoughts behind them made no sense to those who heard them. For several minutes, there was silence. For all their wisdom and cunning, neither Odysseus nor Phoenix could think of anything to say in response. Their good counsel had failed them. But Ajax was neither a man of good counsel nor one of wisdom and cunning. He was a man of action and bloodshed. Throwing aside all that Achilles had said, Ajax spoke directly to him, soldier to soldier:

"Achilles, I know your heart, for it is the same as mine. When the fighting comes close to your tent, you shall join the battle. For now you are too stubborn to listen—the heart within you is as hard and pitiless as bronze—and I for one will waste no more words on you. You are no coward, Achilles. When the time comes, you shall take your sword in your hand and cut a bloody trail through the ranks of the Trojan army."

When Ajax had finished speaking, the children could see that a change had come over Achilles. Ajax had stirred something inside of him, something far deeper and more primal than the words and thoughts that had fallen from his lips.

"Very well, you may tell Agamemnon that I shall remain in my tent until such time as the Trojans should break through to our ships and threaten them with fire. Only then, when my own ships are attacked, shall I put on my armor again and give Hector a taste of my spear."

Achilles sat back down and took up his lyre. As he strummed a sad tune played by shepherds in the hills of Greece, Odysseus, Phoenix, and Ajax quietly left the tent and returned to Agamemnon. Patroclus too returned to his bed, and the children were left alone with Achilles.

"Alex," said Stacey in a hushed voice so that Achilles could not hear her, "the things that Achilles said, weren't they true? If only the others had listened to him, maybe the war would have ended, and the Greeks would have gone home. Can somebody have all the right reasons and still do the wrong thing?"

"You're right, Stacey. The things he said *were* true, but I get ... I get the feeling that he's the first person who ever thought of them. Imagine, Stacey, if you had an idea that could change the whole world and make it better, but you were the first and only person who thought it. Wouldn't everybody think you were crazy? Maybe the world is not yet ready for his ideas. Do you remember, Stacey, when Daddy read us those verses from the Bible? He said that there was a time and a season for everything under the sun: a time for joy and a time for sorrow, a time to live and a time to die, a time for peace and a time for war. Achilles has the right ideas, but it's the wrong time. He's calling for peace, when it's really a time for war."

"Alex, maybe Achilles is a different *kind* of hero."

"What do you mean, Stacey?"

"Well, remember when Hector spoke with Andromache? Everything he said, all the reasons that he gave her for why he had to return to the battlefield were reasons that he had been taught as a child. Cassandra told us that if Hector died, Troy would die too. Maybe that's because Hector *is* Troy. Everything that Troy is and believes in is inside Hector. And I think that if we had met Achilles a week ago, he would have been like Hector: following the rules he learned as a boy and standing for everything that his society stands for. But now Achilles is trying to break away from all the codes and values he was taught. I mean, I could understand Hector, but Achilles is like a riddle."

"Yes, exactly, a riddle. But it's a riddle we must solve, Stacey."

In the background, Achilles continued to play his lyre. The light from the fire cast his shadow on the side of the tent. Alex and Stacey stared at it with eyes wide open. It did not look like the shadow of a man playing a lyre but of a giant holding the world in his hands.

— Chapter —

12

The Counterfeit Achilles

A lex and Stacey rose early the next morning. They hoped that they could speak privately with Achilles before the rest of the camp began a new day of fighting. As they had expected, Achilles was awake. The lyre was still in his hand, and the children wondered if he had slept at all. With their heads bowed, Alex and Stacey walked over to him and sat down at his feet.

"Tell us about your mother, Achilles," said Stacey, "is she really a goddess of the sea? Does that mean she has a fin like a mermaid?"

"No, little one," said Achilles with a laugh, "She has legs just as you and I have. But she is a goddess, and she spends much of her time below the blue waves of the Aegean. I hope you will meet her some day. Everyone loves her. She has a kind heart, but it is very easily wounded. Once when the gods on Mount Olympus captured Zeus and tied him with a rope, Thetis rescued him from his bonds. Once too when Hera grew ashamed of her lame son, Hephaestus (hi FES tus), blacksmith of the gods, and cast him out of Olympus into the sea below, Thetis took him into her cave and tended to his wounds."

"But why did she marry your father, a mortal man?" asked Stacey.

"Ah, that is a tale that has often caused me much pain. It is said that Zeus received a prophecy that a son born to him would overthrow him. Afraid for his throne, Zeus sent spies and messengers throughout the world until they could discover which goddess would bear him such a son. After inflicting great torture on the one who knew the secret (his name was Prometheus, children, but that is another story), Zeus obtained the information. The name of the goddess who would bear him the fated child was Thetis ... yes, that same goddess whom I call mother.

In hopes of escaping the prophecy, Zeus forced Thetis to marry a mortal man and to bear *his* child instead of the child of Zeus. The name of that man was Peleus (PEE lee us), and he it is who is my father. So you see, children, it was my true destiny to be a god: to live forever and to seize some day the very throne of Olympus. Instead, I have been born a man, destined to live my life and then die. Great honor has been taken from me. Zeus knows this, and that is why he granted my mother's prayer on my behalf. I fear now that I spoke that prayer rashly, but it cannot be taken back. Already Zeus has bowed his head and sworn by Styx to fulfill my prayer. Meanwhile, my father waits for me back home and mourns every day, for he knows that I shall never return. Poor Peleus to have such a short-lived son: he, the husband of a goddess, the only mortal to hold his wedding on Mount Olympus."

"The wedding," said Stacey, "the wedding! Is that the wedding where the Golden Apple of Discord was thrown by Eris, the Apple that started this war?"

"Yes, that was the wedding that started it all. Time on Mount Olympus does not always work the same way it does on earth. Months and years have little meaning to beings who live forever. But it pains me to think of such things. Let us speak of something else."

"Achilles," said Alex, changing the subject to a topic that he hoped would help them solve the riddle of Achilles, "did you believe all the things you said last night?"

"Some of them, perhaps all of them. It is hard to say. I was never trained to think about such things. I am not Nestor or Odysseus. Who can I talk to about them? Even Patroclus looks at me as I if were mad."

"I don't think you are mad, Achilles. Someday millions of people will believe the very things you spoke last night. Someday a man will come to the earth who will really be what you almost were. He will teach that all men have equal value and that our worth cannot be measured by things like gold or armor or chariots. He will even tell us that we must love our enemies and pray for those that treat us badly. But Achilles, you are not that man, and you were not meant to be. You are a warrior made for battle. If you wait until the ships are burning, it will be too late. Go now while there is still a chance to stop the killing."

"Yes, the heart within me tells me that you are correct, young Apollo. But I have just sworn to Ajax and the others that I would not return until my ships were in danger. I will not break that oath;

it would shame me before my men. No, my hand has been dealt, and now I must play it to the end."

"No," thought Alex to himself, "No! He sounds just like Priam. There must be a way out of this dilemma. We mustn't just sit back and do nothing. There must be a way!"

Achilles returned to his lyre, and Alex began to pace the room as Patroclus had the night before. Again and again, he ran the problem through his head, but he could find no solution. He walked out to the battlefield and watched the men at war. Things were going worse than they had the day before. As the hours rolled by, Hector led his men on a killing spree. By mid-day, Diomedes and Agamemnon had been struck down by arrows and were too injured to return to battle. By late afternoon, Odysseus himself fell prey to a pike wound. Hector was unstoppable, a superhuman force that no one could resist. Inch by inch, the Trojans pushed the Greeks back to their ships. By early evening, only Ajax and Menelaus were left to lead the troops. The Greeks had earlier built a wall to protect their ships, but it could not hold for much longer. Like a colossus with his legs stretched out, Ajax stood before the wall and refused to move. In his hand he held a thick wooden pike, and with it he smashed the skulls of many a Trojan. But Alex could see that his legs were tiring. He could not last much longer.

Then, like a revelation, the answer flashed through Alex's mind. With the speed of a warrior, Alex raced back to the tent and grabbed Achilles by his shoulders.

"Achilles," he cried, "You will not fight in the battle, very well. But what prevents you from sending someone in your place? When your helmet is on your head and your visor is down, no one can see your face. Let another wear your armor and your helmet and enter into the battle. When the Trojans see your armor, they will think it is you who are fighting, and their spirits will be broken. Please, Achilles, it is our only chance to save the ships."

"Yes, I agree to your plan, but who shall wear my armor and fight in my place?"

"I will Achilles," said a voice behind them. It was Patroclus. He had been hiding in the shadows and had heard their conversation.

"Patroclus, you alone shall wear my armor and fight in my place. But you must promise me now, old friend, that once you have caused panic in the Trojan army and have given the Greeks a chance to recover and regroup that you will return here to me. Whatever happens, you must not go after Hector yourself, or you will be killed."

"Yes, Achilles you have my word. But quick, we have no time to waste. Help me to put on your armor that I may rescue the ships from danger."

A week of idleness had not slowed the reflexes of Achilles. He immediately sprang to his feet and, with the help of the children, clothed Patroclus in his magnificent armor: armor that had been given to his father as a wedding present by the gods and which Peleus in turn had given to his son.

First, they strapped along his legs the strong greaves studded with silver. The moment they touched his legs, Patroclus felt the blood rush to his face, and he was filled with a fiery courage. Next, they slung around his chest the bronze corselet that had repelled a hundred arrows from the noble heart of the son of Peleus. From his shoulder they hung the sword belt and sword, and upon his arm they laid the mighty shield. Over his head they placed the helmet with its crest of horsehair, and they drew down the visor so that no one could see his face. But one part of the armor of Achilles was not given to him. He could not carry the great ash spear of Peleus for such was its weight and length that no man but Achilles could wield it. Instead, two spears were given him to hold in each hand, spears with which he would tear open the flesh of many Trojans.

"Remember your promise," said Achilles and pushed Patroclus out of the tent. Three times Patroclus bent his knees and felt the armor rattle on his body. Three times he lifted the spears above his head and swung them in the air. Then, with a great war cry that shook the earth beneath him, he charged into the battle. The Greek soldiers who saw him shouted with joy and stepped aside to let him pass. Faster and faster he ran, until those he passed could barely see him. But the Trojans saw and terror seized their hearts. They all knew the shield and the crest of Achilles. Though Hector called to them to stand their ground, they broke their ranks and scattered in fear.

Just as a wolf stalks the hills until he sees a flock of sheep in the valley below, and then falls upon them with great speed, now tearing the throat of one, now biting the leg of another; all day through the field he ranges so that not a single sheep escapes from his fangs and so that their blood lies thick on the grass. Just so, the Trojans fled before Patroclus like sheep before a wolf, but none of them could escape his spears and his sword. Slashing and stabbing in every direction, Patroclus pushed back the Trojan army until he saw rising up before him the Walls of Troy.

It was the Trojans now and not the Greeks who were desperate to defend their home territory. For a split second, Patroclus lifted his visor and stared at the wall. He saw that it was bent inward slightly, and a mad idea seized him. With a speed that even the swift-footed Achilles would be hard-pressed to match, Patroclus ran toward the wall. He hit the bottom with his left foot and pushed himself upward and forward. His right foot hit the wall higher up and then his left foot higher still. His speed defied gravity itself, and his body rose upward toward the top of the wall. And now, Patroclus might have scaled the wall and brought destruction to the city of Troy, but that honor was not to be his. The Trojans beat him back, and he fell to earth.

As he felt the ground beneath him again, a voice within him cried out: "Remember your promise to Achilles. You have broken the spirit of the Trojans and saved the Greek ships. Now you must return."

But another voice rose up beside the first. It was that of the Accuser: "Foolish boy. Now is your chance to show how great you are. Why should Achilles win the honor of killing Hector? You are as strong and as brave as Achilles. Have you not single-handedly driven the Trojan army back to their city wall? Do not give up the honor that is due to you alone. The armor you wear is just armor. It is *your* strength and greatness that has saved the day. Achilles only made you promise so that he would have the chance to steal your glory and your prize."

Normally, the gentle Patroclus would never have listened to such words. But he was no longer Patroclus. Wearing the armor of Achilles and seeing the Trojans flee before him had made him believe that he *was* Achilles, that he could not be defeated, that he would live forever. The blood was pounding in his ears, blocking out both pity and good counsel. He would not give up his chance for glory. He would take on Hector himself.

This was a turn of events that Alex had not foreseen. But there was nothing he could do, nothing that anyone could do. Patroclus turned his back to the wall and looked out over the battlefield. Hector was racing toward him with his spear held high over his head. As he ran, Greek and Trojan alike moved backward, away from the center of the field. Soon, Patroclus and Hector stood alone, glaring angrily at each other over the blood-stained grass. For a moment, everything froze, and it seemed to Alex that he could almost hear the sound of the grass growing and the trees putting forth leaves.

Then… *snap*, their swords flashed out and clanged heavily on the shield of their opponent. At first, Patroclus had the upper hand. Three times his sword beat down on Hector's shield and drove the Trojan warrior to his knees. But Hector was not to be overpowered so easily. The next time Patroclus brought down his sword, he pushed his shield up and to the side. The force knocked the sword out of Patroclus' hand and sent it soaring through the air. As Patroclus bent down to retrieve his weapon, Hector too bent down and lifted a massive stone from the earth. Six men, such as they are today, would be hard pressed to move such a stone together, but Hector, with godlike strength, lifted it over his head and threw it at his Greek enemy. The rock struck Patroclus where the thighbone connects with the hip and tore it out of joint. Even so, as he fell, he cast his spear at the son of Priam. But the gods were with Hector that day, and the wind blew the spear so that it only grazed him on the neck.

Clutching his leg with his right hand, dizzy with pain, Patroclus reached up with his left and removed his helmet. If die he must, he would do it with his eyes clear. Seeing the bare head of Patroclus, Hector was taken aback, and he slowly returned his sword to its sheath. But as he thought to himself of all the fine Trojans that Patroclus had slain (one of them a son of Zeus by a mortal woman), he drew it out again. A dark, sinister laugh slipped through his teeth—not at all like the laugh Alex and Stacey had heard him make on the watchtower of Troy—and he began to taunt the fallen warrior:

"So you thought yourself the equal of Achilles, did you? You thought that by wearing his armor you could defeat even me? Where now is your borrowed courage and your counterfeit strength? No, my dear impostor, it is *you* who shall feel the sting of *my* blade. With my sword I shall draw out your spirit and send it flying to Hades. Then shall I strip Achilles' armor from your corpse and wear it myself."

"Kill me if you must, Hector, but know this of a certainty: I shall not be two days in Hades before your spirit follows in my wake. Even so, I do not think that you shall kill me so easily."

The pain in his leg was almost beyond endurance, but still Patroclus managed to raise himself on to his side and hold up his shield. With a sharp twist of his arm, he was even able to block the first blow of Hector's sword. But the movement drained away all of his remaining energy. He sank back to the earth, and his shield fell at his side. Hector found a bare spot in the armor and thrust his sword into Patroclus' neck. The warrior groaned once, and then his body went limp. As swift as a moonbeam that falls to the earth on a cloudless night, the soul of Patroclus flew downward to the house of the dead. And as it flew, it mourned for its lost youth and for the bitter destiny that had dragged it, all unwilling, to its doom.

Alex and Stacey hugged each other tightly and cried until there were no tears left inside of them. Though they had known him for only a day, they had already come to love the gentle Patroclus. But their tears were not for him alone. They wept too for Hector, for the bitterness that must have seized his heart and driven him to kill the injured Patroclus. How horrible that two men such as these, kind and noble, should allow anger and revenge and the fury of war to cause them to forget the virtues that made them human. The words of Pan returned to them and rang in their ears: it was not war itself that was evil but the emptiness and misery it often led to. They understood now what Pan meant when he said that the Accuser was anti-life and anti-joy. He had stolen life and joy, not just from Patroclus, but from Hector as well.

Such thoughts pressed heavily on Alex and Stacey as they mourned the death of their friend. But upon Alex, the weight was heaviest. He had been the one who had suggested that Patroclus fight in the place of Achilles. He, therefore, and he alone, would have to be the one to tell Achilles the news of his friend's death.

— Chapter —

13

Creation and Destruction

Sitting alone in the darkness of his tent, Achilles did not yet know the fate of Patroclus. But he could hear the shouts from the battlefield, and the spirit within him groaned aloud at the thought that Patroclus had forgotten his promise and gone after Hector. Behind him, he heard the parting of the curtains that hung at the entrance of his tent, and felt the presence of someone standing beside him in the dark.

"What is the news from the field?" he asked.

"Patroclus has saved us," said Alex, "The Trojans have fled in fear, and our ships are out of danger. He fought bravely and well, Achilles. You would have been proud."

"What are you hiding from me, boy? Tell me the truth, all of it."

Alex took a deep breath and closed his eyes. The truth poured out of him in a rush of words: "Patroclus is dead, Achilles. Hector killed him and stripped off his armor. Even now, the Greeks are fighting to get back his body from the Trojans."

Achilles cried out in pain, a cry that seemed to come from deep within him and that sounded to Alex more like the scream of a hawk or a wolf than that of a man. He dug his fingers into the ground and filled his hands with black dirt. Crying out all the while, he smeared the dirt on his hair and his face until his once noble features grew dark and muddied. As Alex watched with horror, he thought of the books he had read about the wars fought between cowboys and Indians. Before the Indians fought a battle, their warriors would smear their faces with red and black war paint. Some did this, Alex remembered, to transform themselves into a ferocious spirit or animal. It was not they but the mask that would bring death to their enemy. Just so, Achilles in his grief was transforming himself into something not quite human.

"Patroclus," he cried, "Patroclus! What sorrow has fallen upon me! Never again will I see you coming to me from across the battlefield. Never again shall we fight together or share a cup of wine in victory. Now death has taken you away, and I was not near to rescue you."

As he continued to cry out in his pain, calling again and again upon the spirit of Patroclus, Alex saw a great marvel. The ground near Achilles seemed to move and sway as though it were made of water. Here and there, white specks danced above the ground. It looked to Alex like the white crest on the top of a breaking wave or like the flecks of foam that are washed up on the shore. The specks of white began to swirl, and, as they did, they took on a shape that almost seemed human. One moment, there was nothing there but sparkling dust; the next a woman lay on the ground beside the weeping Achilles.

"O my son," the woman cried, "Surely you are the most short-lived of all men. But why do you weep so? Has all not happened as you prayed for? Have not the finest warriors of Greece fallen before the spear of Hector? Will the Greeks not come now to your tent and beg you to return and save them? Speak to me what is in your heart."

"Mother, all my joy has left me, and nothing remains but sorrow. My friend and kinsman has fallen, while I sit here in my tent, a useless weight on the green earth. Oh why did the gods of Olympus ever drive you into the arms of a mortal man? Better that you had remained childless all your days than to bring such a son into the world. There is nothing left for me now but to take from Hector his accursed life."

"Beware, my son," said Thetis, "for it is fated that if you kill Hector, your own death will follow soon after."

"What do I care for my life or for anything else but the blood of Hector on my spear? First I shall avenge my friend, and then what does it matter what follows. I have grown sick of life. This child here was right when he told me that I was a soldier. What have I to do with thinking and good counsel? I reject with hatred all the words that I spoke before Odysseus and the others. My hunger now is only for the blood and groans of men."

"No, Achilles," said Alex, springing to his feet, "That is not the answer. Do not go from one extreme to the other. My father once told me that the Greeks of old valued four virtues above all others:

courage, justice, wisdom, and self-control. The first two you have, Achilles: your courage and your justice are great indeed. But you lack the second two. Be wise, Achilles, and control your great anger. If you rush now onto the battlefield without shield or armor, some Trojan will kill you with an arrow or a spear. At least wait until you can find new armor; by then, perhaps, your anger and wrath will have cooled down."

"Again, you speak with wisdom, young Apollo. But where am I to find armor as great as that given to me by Peleus?"

"I know," said Stacey, who had followed Alex into the tent and who had been standing listening for some time now, "I know where you can get the finest armor of all. Thetis, your son told us that you once helped Hephaestus, the blacksmith of the gods. Perhaps if we go to him now, he will remember your kindness to him and make Achilles a set of armor like no man has ever worn."

"Yes, mother, you must take these children with you and go at once to the workshop of the Lord of Fire. But first, I must do what I can to help the men who are fighting to get back the body of the fallen Patroclus."

Before anyone could stop him, Achilles, without armor or weapons of any kind, ran from the tent and stood at the edge of the battlefield. Then, raising up his arms and lifting his head skyward, he let out a mighty battle cry. Three times, Achilles lifted his arms; three times he let forth his cry. Straightaway, five of the finest Trojan chariots ran headlong into the mud, and their drivers were thrown in the air and dashed against the rocks. Terror seized the hearts of the Trojans, and then and there, six warriors threw themselves on their own spears and perished. Panic ran throughout the Trojan camp, and the Greeks rushed in and rescued the body of Patroclus.

The body was brought to Achilles who held it in his arms and wept warm tears. He ordered his maidservants to wash down the body with expensive oils and perfumes, while Achilles himself gathered wood for a pyre.

But neither Alex nor Stacey saw any of this, for by now, they were traveling, like two twin dolphins, under the blue waters of the Aegean. Thetis held the children under her arms as if they were two great loaves of bread, and they found, to their astonishment, that they could breathe in the water as if it were air. They looked beneath them and saw, spread out as upon a magic carpet, the wonders of the ocean floor. Mermaids and mermen swam in and out of hidden reefs never before seen by human eyes. Fish that wore the colors of the rainbow on their backs brushed by Stacey's arm, while Alex felt, wrapped around his leg, the long tail of a giant stingray. Suddenly everything went dark, and the children closed their eyes in fear. Though they did not know it, they were being taken through a secret, underground river that led straight to the heart of a volcano.

With a rush of air that caused the children to open their eyes again, they and Thetis leapt out of the water and landed on a sand dune. Though the light was dim and had a reddish glow to it, Alex and Stacey could tell immediately that they were in some kind of a cave. Too awe-struck to speak, they stood and followed Thetis silently as she walked out of the narrow cave into a large cavern with high rock walls and stalactites that stretched down from a cathedral-like ceiling. In the center of the cavern, a huge fire sent red and blue flames shooting in every direction. From two hundred feet away, the children could feel its heat and turned their faces to the side in fear that their skin would catch on fire. It was twenty times hotter than the bonfire they had once attended at Daddy's University.

It made Alex think of the story of the phoenix: of that magical bird that lived for a thousand years, and then flew to the top of the highest mountain in the world where it built itself a massive funeral pyre. When the fire was as hot as a thousand furnaces, the phoenix would fly high in the air and then swoop down into the center of the pyre where he would be burnt to a crisp. But then, magically, the ashes of the bird would swirl in the fire and recombine, and out of the flames a new phoenix would spring and begin its own solitary, thousand-year existence. The story was one of Alex and Stacey's favorites. Indeed, Daddy had told it to them so many times that they had it all but memorized by now.

But *this* fire, hot as it was, had clearly not been built by a bird. As their eyes grew accustomed to the glare, Alex and Stacey picked out the figure of a man crouching over the fire and holding two hammers in his hands. He was really more giant than man; the muscles that bulged on his arms were themselves as big as a normal man's head. Aside from sandals and a towel that he wore wrapped around his waist like a Scottish kilt, the man was naked—or almost naked. From the top of his head to the tops of his feet, he was completely covered with a thick mat of dark, wavy hair. Large drops of sweat poured down from his forehead and chest, and the children could see by the way he moved that he was slightly hunchbacked and lame in one leg.

Alex and Stacey had once gone to a festival where they had seen a real blacksmith at work. They remembered that he had a bellows which he used to squeeze air on to the fire and thus make it burn more brightly. This blacksmith, whom the children knew at once must be Hephaestus, also had a bellows, but he never touched it with his hands. Rather, when he needed more air for his fire, he spoke to the bellows, and it moved by itself. In the same way, whenever he needed a tool, he merely spoke its name and it flew into his hand. To help him in his work, he was attended upon by three lovely maidservants who seemed to shine in the glow of the fire. Alex and Stacey soon learned why; they were made completely of gold!

As the children continued to stare in wonder, Thetis put some lotion on her hands and spread it thickly over their faces and arms and legs. The lotion, she explained, would protect them from the heat and allow them to stand close to Hephaestus as he worked. Happy to learn that they were now safe from being burned, Alex and Stacey carefully approached the fire and the blacksmith who stood over it. He had just pulled a sword out of the flames and was beating it into shape on his anvil. The sound of his hammer as it beat on the metal was like that of a drum, and to the rhythm of that "metal drum" Hephaestus sang:

> The swords I make are used to kill,
> I know this and it pains me,
> But even so I make them still,
> My destiny constrains me.

> To me alone Olympus gave
> The secret of the fire;
> To use that gift is all I crave,
> It is my one desire.

> While battle shakes the Walls of Troy,
> I stand still at my station;
> Let soldiers slaughter and destroy,
> My calling is creation.

And so I forge the sword and knife,
  Each one a thing of beauty;
To bring such treasures into life
  Forever is my duty.

So engrossed was Hephaestus in his work and his song that it took him several minutes to realize that three people were standing at his back. However, the moment he did, he put down his hammers and turned to greet his visitors. Normally, he would have treated any guest who came to his workshop with cheerful hospitality, but when he saw that his visitors included the goddess Thetis, his face shown with extra delight.

The children thought he would never stop hugging and kissing them and praising Thetis for her kind heart and lovely face. And when they had finished the epic meal that the God of Fire had spread out before them, Alex and Stacey felt like two whales that had been washed up on the shore and were too heavy to roll back into the water. It was all so delightful that for a full hour they forgot the tragedy that had impelled them to visit Hephaestus in his fiery cavern. But the urgency of their mission soon returned to their minds, and Thetis addressed Hephaestus with heavy words:

"Alas, I wish the reason for our visit had been a happy one, but I come to you now in great pain and need." And from there, Thetis went on to tell him all that had transpired in the Greek camp from the argument between Achilles and Agamemnon to the death of Patroclus and the stealing of his borrowed armor. Hephaestus listened in silence, a look of sorrow on his face. When Thetis had done, the lame blacksmith of the gods took her hand in his and spoke to her gently. Of all the gods on Mount Olympus only he was imperfect in body, yet to Stacey, he seemed for a moment the most handsome god of all.

"Dearest Thetis," he said, "I wish that I could pull your son out of the battle and bring him back to Greece where he would live a long life by your side. But such power has not been given to me. Still, I will do what I can. Like you, Thetis, I fear that Achilles' days on the earth are numbered. So be it, if that is the will of Zeus. But I swear by Styx, good lady, that if die he must, he will die with glory. I shall make for him the finest suit of armor that has ever graced the body of a mortal warrior. In his hands he will bear a spear and a shield the like of which no man has ever seen or ever shall see again. Though destruction stands all around him, I shall use my arts—the arts of creation—to bring beauty and grace into the very midst of death and despair."

"Yes," said Alex, rising from his seat and standing by the side of Thetis, "You have found another way, Lord Hephaestus, to fight the Accuser. Like Hector's laugh, your arts are a thing that the Accuser can neither defeat nor understand. Even though our father is a teacher, he taught us once that we should respect those who work with their hands. I see now what he meant. There is a kind of magic in work that can lift us up almost to the level of the gods."

"For one so young," said Hephaestus, "you have much wisdom. Work is indeed magic, as are all the arts by which man gives form and shape to the chaos around him. The armor I make today for Achilles shall endure long after Troy has fallen and all the warriors of Greece have gone to their graves. It shall remain a thing to delight the eyes of many generations to come.

"But I shall do more than this. On the shield, I shall engrave the shapes and figures of two cities. In the one there shall be weddings and festivals and the seasons that turn endlessly on their wheel.

There you shall see those who plant and those who reap and those who make wine from the juice of the grape. But in the other, there shall be war and treachery and wrath. Young men shall slaughter other young men, and the fields will be choked with blood. Instruct Achilles and all others who look on the shield to heed well its warning. The two cities represent the choice that is laid out before each of us. Let us pray that we all choose the right city.

"But now the three of you must lie here on the ground and sleep. I shall be working with such speed and fury that most of the air in this cavern will be consumed by the fire. When the armor has been completed, I shall wake you and send you back to the tent of Achilles."

Almost immediately, Alex and Stacey fell into a deep sleep and dreamed a wild dream. They were surrounded on all sides by a wall of fire, but they were not afraid of the flames. They reached out their hands and put them in the fire, and when they drew them back, their hands seemed stronger and purer than before. They looked deep into the fire and saw it surge and flow like waves that roll back and forth on a sandy beach. Alex and Stacey had once built a sandcastle on the shore of Lake Michigan and then had watched sadly as the tide rose and slowly destroyed it. Now, as they stared more deeply into the flames, they were carried back in their dream to that very shore. They watched again the waves break on the beach, but this time, marvel of marvels, each time the wave touched the sand it formed another section of the sandcastle. By the fifth wave, their sandcastle had been restored; by the tenth, it had grown into a palace with high towers and an intricate courtyard. The water became fire again, and out of the fire, cities and nations rose and grew.

"Wake, my friends!" said Hephaestus, and shook each of them with his large, sinewy hands. "The work is done! Achilles longs for your return. You must not delay. Farewell."

Darkness at Noon

In the heroic, legendary world of Homer's Troy, the dawn means more, and *is* more, than the rising of the sun. The dawn is, in fact, a lovely goddess with wings on her back and a circle of golden fire about her head. Her name is Eos (EE os), and she has the loveliest, finest fingers of any woman who ever lived. Each finger is long and slender and glows with the color of a newly-budded, dew-drenched rose. When Thetis and the children returned to the tent of Achilles, Eos was in the very process of spreading out her rosy fingers across the morning sky. The warriors of Greece and Troy were rising from their beds and putting on their armor for another terrible day of battle.

But Achilles did not rise, for he had never slept. All night he had paced his tent, awaiting the time when his mother would bring him his new armor. Though the other Greeks had begged him to sleep and to eat, he had refused to do either until the body of Hector lay dead under his spear. It would have been better, perhaps, had Alex and Stacey remained with Achilles while Thetis went to the workshop of Hephaestus. For awhile, Alex's words about the four virtues, especially wisdom and self-control, had calmed Achilles' raging spirit, but when the children left and the soldiers retired to their beds, the memories of his days with Patroclus came back fresh in his mind and carried with them bloody thoughts of anger and revenge.

At the moment of his mother's return, Achilles was outside of the tent staring longingly at the battlefield where men win glory. In his mind's eye he could already see the grass covered with the bodies of the men he would kill that day. Whatever wrath he had previously felt against Agamemnon had now been transferred to Hector. But it was no simple shift from one to the other. In moving from Agamemnon to Hector, Achilles' wrath had multiplied a hundredfold. All of Achilles' hatreds and fears—his obsession with his own death, his sense of frustration that he had been born a mortal instead of a god, his feelings of guilt over the death of Patroclus, and his utter rejection of his new ideas about honor and value—all these he now directed against the Trojan Prince. Hector would be made to pay, not only for Patroclus' death, but for all the strife and confusion that was tearing in two the heart of the great Achilles.

After rejecting the words of the Accuser and choosing instead the path of virtue, Hercules had gone on to rid Greece of all of the beasts and monsters that raged outside the city walls. But there was one beast he could not kill: the beast that rages within the human breast. That battle was being waged now inside the heart and soul of Achilles. The outcome of that battle would determine the very shape of Western civilization. To help Achilles win this battle against the Accuser within, to help him choose the path of virtue, joy, and life—for this reason, Alex and Stacey had been brought back from the future.

Behind him, Achilles heard the sound of movement in his tent. Immediately he rushed in and greeted his mother with an anxious embrace.

"Have you brought it, mother? Has Hephaestus made me armor that can outshine in glory and strength that given to me by Peleus?"

"It is all that and more, my son. In this armor, and with these weapons, you shall shine like the God of War himself. Nothing shall stand in your path, and no weapon forged by man shall harm you. But come, let us help you to put on these gifts from the God of Fire."

Just as they had dressed Patroclus the day before, so now Alex and Stacey helped to fasten the greaves and the corselet and the helmet to the body of Achilles. When they were done, the warrior took up his mighty shield and stepped out of the tent. As he did, the sun fell upon it and sent bright rays of light shooting in every direction.

"Achilles, my son," said Thetis, "see how the sun blazons from your shield as though it were a lighthouse that guides sailors home through stormy seas. So may your shield and the choice engraved upon it be like a lighthouse to guide you home. Now go, my son, and fulfill your destiny. Though my heart is sore, I shall not stand in your way."

By the time Achilles had donned his armor and stepped out of his tent, the day's battle had begun. Trojan and Greek faced each other across the field, their spears extended. The army of Troy had regrouped after the assault of Patroclus and, inspired by a speech from Hector, was once again threatening the Greek ships. All of that was about to change.

As coal is shoveled into the furnace, and the fire blazes red hot sending forth steam to drive the pistons, and the engine groans and lurches forward building up speed with each turn of the wheel until the train hurtles down the track; so the heart of swift-footed Achilles sent blood flowing into his legs, and his powerful knees began pumping up and down, driving his feet against the ground and propelling his body faster and faster across the field. A chariot drawn by four horses could scarcely move as quickly as Achilles did over the blood-stained grass. With one graceful motion, he pulled his sword from its sheath and brandished it in the air. Without once breaking his stride, he drew his sword back and forth against the necks of a dozen Trojans. Men fell in his path as grain before the reaper when the harvest is gathered in.

After another dozen Trojans had fallen victim to his sword, Achilles, still running, found himself by the river Scamander (sca MAN der), which flowed down from the foothills of Mount Ida and wrapped itself around and through the plain of Troy. Anxious to end his deadly charge, an entire troop of Trojan soldiers had pursued Achilles to the river, where they hoped to ambush and kill him. Achilles, sensing their presence behind him, stopped dead in his tracks and turned to face them. With a shout, the Trojans rushed upon him, their swords held high. Achilles neither moved nor spoke. For the next hour, he drove his sword, one by one, into their sides and shoulders and thighs. With each new kill, he grabbed the slain warrior and tossed his corpse into the river behind him. Soon, the Scamander was so thick with the bodies of men that its waters could barely flow. In desperation, the god of the river called out to Achilles:

"Achilles, are you mad? Stop this slaughter or you will choke me with blood. In your anger and wrath, you have defiled me."

But the warrior was not to be held back by man or god. With one giant leap, Achilles threw himself into the center of the river and continued his bloody work. Enraged that his warning had not been heeded, the god of the river rose up in a wave and attempted to drown Achilles. In response, he merely planted his feet more firmly in the river bed and began to slash at the wave with his sword. It was a strange sight indeed, this battle of man against nature, but then the man who waged it was no ordinary man. After many minutes, Achilles grew tired of the contest, and leapt back out onto the dry land. Why should he waste his time fighting immortal river gods when there were still Trojans left to kill?

By now, Achilles had slaughtered every soldier who had pursued him down to the Scamander and was preparing himself for a direct attack on the wall. And then he saw him, a lone figure making his way past the river toward the main gate of Troy. Achilles recognized him at once. His name was Lycaon (LICK un), and he was a son of King Priam. Many years earlier, Achilles had captured him in battle and had sold him as a slave in return for a great ransom. Now, after making a long search, Priam had finally found his lost son and had redeemed him from his bitter slavery. Even now, the young man was heading for home to be reunited with his family.

"Lycaon," said Achilles, grabbing the young man and pushing him to the ground, "it was unwise of you to cross my path again. This time you shall surely not escape my sword."

"Please, Achilles, have pity on me. I beg you in the name of your own father, Peleus, who waits for you back in Greece. My father, Priam, will pay you a great ransom if you return me to the palace alive. Have pity on me, Achilles, who have suffered so much already at your hand. I am at your knees, a helpless suppliant."

In the past, Achilles would have heeded such a plea and sold his captive for a noble ransom. Indeed, it was precisely for such ransom that the soldiers fought. But not today. Even as Lycaon made his plea, Achilles pressed his foot upon the young man's chest and poised his sword above his neck. He then spoke out in a voice without pity:

"In the past, Lycaon, it was the way of my heart to be merciful and to release from death all those Trojans who fell beneath the sway of my sword. But that time is past. No one who falls beneath my blade shall escape death, especially not if they come from the house of Priam. Why do you squirm beneath my foot? What matter if I should end your life? Patroclus is dead, who was by far a better man than you; even I, who claim a goddess as my mother, will someday know the sting of death and the dark journey to the underworld. So why all this fuss? Die now, and in the days to come, let all die such a death until Patroclus is avenged."

"Yes, Achilles, we all shall die. Then let us gain glory before we do. No glory can come of your killing me; neither shall any ransom come to your tent. Look at me, I am defenseless. In killing me, you will not even win armor to display before your men."

"You speak rightly, Lycaon, when you say that we all shall die. Then let us get on with it, I say. Speak not to me of glory and of prizes; the only prize I desire now is the life of Hector who stole from me my dearest companion."

Thus spoke Achilles and thrust his sword into the bare chest of Lycaon. At once, his soul flew from his body and was dragged screaming to Hades. Achilles pressed his foot down near where the sword had entered Lycaon's chest. Grabbing the hilt and twisting it to the side, he pulled out the sword and returned it, still red with blood, to its sheath.

It was a terrible deed, one that ran contrary to the heroic code that Achilles and Hector had learned as boys, but it provided for the Trojans a needed breathing space. As Achilles spoke his grim words to Lycaon, all the Trojans still left alive on the battlefield ran for the Scaean Gates and the safety of the Trojan Wall. All the Trojans, that is, but one.

When Achilles reached the base of the wall, he found to his great anger that no Trojans were left on the field. Like a ram butting his head against a tree, Achilles struck the wall with his bare fist, and it seemed to those above that he would tear it apart, brick by brick. But something stayed his hand before it could strike a second time. Out of the corner of his eye, Achilles caught sight of a single Trojan still standing outside the wall. It was Hector. Driven partly mad by his own bloodlust and desire for vengeance against the Greeks, Hector had refused to run inside with his men. From the watchtower above him, his mother and father had called to him in sorrow, begging him to come in the city and be safe. But Hector had deafened himself to their cries.

Now, as he stood alone awaiting the approach of Achilles, Hector wished within that he had listened to the pleas of Priam and Hecuba. The very second he caught sight of Hector, Achilles had begun to run, faster and faster, at the enemy he hated so fiercely. For a moment, Hector held his ground, but when he saw on the face of Achilles the pitiless, unyielding look of Hades himself, his spirit was overcome by fear, and he turned and ran. Three times, swift-footed Achilles chased Hector around the Walls of Troy as Greek and Trojan alike looked on in stunned silence. The air itself grew still, and the birds ceased their singing. Even Olympus held its breath, too shocked and awe-struck to move or intervene.

As Stacey watched with horror this race for the life of Hector, she wanted to yell out to him that he should stop running, turn to Achilles, and offer to give back Helen. But she did not do so. She knew within that such an action would be futile: it would not save Hector from Achilles' sword. The war was no longer about Helen, just as Achilles' wrath was no longer tied to the stubborn folly of Agamemnon. The stakes were higher now. The game would have to be played to the end.

Perhaps you have had a nightmare in which an evil man or a wild beast is chasing you through a forest or over a long field. You run as quickly as you can, run and run until your heart is pounding in your chest and the sweat drips down your forehead and into your eyes. You run until your lungs come near to bursting, and yet still you feel the breath of the enemy on your neck. Then, suddenly, the dream changes. Everything goes into slow motion. Still you run with all the strength that is within you, but it is as if you are running through mud or through a sticky pool of black syrup. The enemy too slows in its pursuit so that it does not overtake you, yet remains ever at your heels. So was it now for Hector. Achilles could not catch him, yet neither could Hector break away. It was as if they, and the whole world around them, were caught in a dream from which there was no escape. The sun hung still in the noonday sky, and blinded the two warriors with its burning rays.

"No!" shouted Hector, and the sound of his voice shattered the dream-state into which all the onlookers had been lulled. "I will no longer run from you, Achilles. If kill me you must, your spear shall pierce my chest, not my back."

As he spoke these words, Hector stopped dead in his tracks and turned to face his pursuer. Achilles too stopped and glared maliciously at the Trojan Prince over a thirty-foot space of grass.

"Wait, Achilles," said Hector, "Before our swords meet, let us make a pact. If I kill you, I shall take your armor, but your body I will not defile. Rather, I shall return it with all honor to your Greek companions. So, Achilles, do you the same. If you should take my life in battle, strip my armor from me, but have pity on my poor corpse. Return it to my family that they may give it proper burial."

"Hector, most hateful of all men, there are no pacts between wolves. Lions and bears do not enter into vows before they take their prey. So neither will I make you any promises. By the gods, if I could, I would tear out your liver and eat it raw."

Stacey had never before heard such cruel and hateful words. She thought to herself that they must be the words of the Accuser. But she was wrong. The words were Achilles'. For one terrible moment, Achilles had *become* the Accuser.

"What injury have I done you, Achilles, that you hate me thus?"

"I will waste no more words on you. Feel instead the point of my spear."

Taking in his hand the great ash spear of Peleus, Achilles drew it back over his shoulder and hurled it at Hector. It smashed into the breastplate, splitting the bronze in half but leaving the flesh of Hector unharmed.

"Not so easily shall you send me to Hades, great Achilles," said Hector, and cast his own spear at the head of the Greek warrior. Had the helmet been that of any other man, the blow would have been fatal, but the helmet that now covered the head of Achilles had been forged by Hephaestus himself. The spear neither pierced nor scratched the helmet, but bounced off uselessly and fell on the grass.

Hector knew then that this was a battle he could not win, but he pledged to himself that before he died, he would do one last great deed. Drawing his sword, he charged headlong at Achilles. Sword, arm, and body moved together in a single deadly stroke that would have knocked even the great Ajax to his knees. Achilles caught the stroke full on his shield; the Walls of Troy and even the foothills of Mount Ida trembled at the sound. But the son of Peleus remained standing.

Like a hawk that spots its prey and then dives swiftly to earth, Achilles swooped down on Hector. His sword slashed through the air so quickly that it seemed to light it on fire. Hector countered with his shield, but the force of the blow threw him on his back. Achilles looked down on him and searched for the spot that he alone knew: the one weakness in the armor given to him by his father, Peleus. There, near the base of the corselet, a gap in the armor, barely visible to the eye. There now, into that gap, Achilles thrust his sword. The point split open the belly of Hector and warm blood ran onto the grass.

"Achilles," cried Hector, "you have defeated me. Return me now to my father, and he will give you great ransom. Or if you will not, swear at least that you will give back my corpse."

"Not if you gave me three times your own weight in gold would I spare your life. And think not that you shall be buried with honor. I shall keep your body myself to give it as food to the beasts of the field and the birds of the air."

"Beware, Achilles. If you kill me now, your own death will follow shortly."

"So be it," said Achilles, and drove his sword once again into the belly of Hector. The warrior groaned once, and then his body went limp. As swift as a moonbeam that falls to the earth on a cloudless night, the soul of Hector flew downward to the house of the dead. And as it flew, it mourned for its lost youth and for the bitter destiny that had dragged it, all unwilling, to its doom.

Achilles drew out his blade and whirled it victoriously in the air. A great war cry broke forth from his lips and cut through the air with the same ferocity as his blade. In full view of Greek and Trojan alike, Achilles stripped the armor from Hector and tossed his naked corpse on the earth. But even this act of defilement did not satisfy Achilles. With the sharp edge of a knife, he pierced holes in Hector's lifeless ankles and, with great thongs of leather, attached the body to the back of his chariot. Then, as the family of Hector looked on helplessly from the watchtower, Achilles drove the chariot three times around the Walls of Troy. It was a ghastly sight indeed, one that I shall not even try to describe to you. Suffice it to say that the sun itself refused to look upon it and closed its golden eye until the bloody deed had been accomplished.

The wailing that rose that day from Priam and Hecuba alone was enough to break the heart of the strongest of men. Alex and Stacey wept with them as they had wept the day before for Patroclus. It did not matter now that one was Greek and the other a Trojan: the sorrow and the tragedy were the same.

But as the children cast their eyes up to the tower, they noticed that there was one member of Hector's family who was absent. Nowhere did they see the lovely face of the gentle Andromache. And well they did not, for at that moment, Hector's loving and dutiful wife was in the very place he had asked her to be. Stationed in the center of her chamber, Andromache worked away at her loom. In her hand, she held a shuttle, and with that shuttle she wove her silver thread in and out of a great and beautiful tapestry.

Busy at her work, she knew nothing of what was happening outside the walls of her city. But when the wailing rose from the watchtower and the cries of Hecuba reached her ears, Andromache knew in her heart that Hector was no more. A cold chill ran through her body, and the shuttle dropped from her hand. Stitch by stitch the tapestry began to unweave. And as it did, it seemed to Andromache that just so had the subtle fabric that was the life of Hector come unstrung. Troy too was such a fabric, and it would not be long now before the city itself unraveled before her eyes.

— Chapter —
15

The Proper Way to Grieve

Earlier that year, Alex and Stacey had attended the funeral of their great-grandmother. It was the first funeral they had ever attended, and they had studied carefully the reactions of their relatives. As children, the concept of grieving did not mean much to them, and they were eager to understand how one was to react and behave in such a situation. They noted that each person, from their grandfather to their mother to their aunts and uncles, had reacted differently. Some cried loudly and lifted their hands in the air; others bowed their heads and let quiet tears fall from their eyes; yet others stood motionless, their eyes unblinking, as if they were trying their best to prevent a single tear from falling. Some talked a great deal, while others spoke not a word. Some paced the room, while others sat in chairs or huddled together in tight groups. When it was all over, Alex and Stacey decided that there wasn't one single "right way" to grieve.

Now, as they watched Achilles in his grief, they learned a new lesson. Although there may be more than one right way to grieve, there certainly are wrong ways. The children had felt sure that once Achilles had taken his revenge on Hector, he would slowly return to normal and his crushing grief for Patroclus would pass. But now it seemed that the very opposite had taken place. The death of Hector had only fueled his grief, causing it to grow and swell in intensity.

As they and the entire Greek camp watched in disbelief, Achilles continued to weep for Patroclus and to smear his face with dirt and ashes. He continued in his refusal to sleep or eat and could be found at any hour of the day or night pacing the shore and crying out in pain. When he did lie down in his tent, he would toss and turn violently: now lying on his side, now on his back, now again on his stomach. After an hour of this, he would jump back to his feet and pace again the sandy shore. At times, when his grief was most desperate, he would tie Hector's corpse to his chariot and drag it around and around the funeral pyre he had built for Patroclus. But still, Achilles found no relief for his pain or his sorrow.

By now, everyone in the camp knew that Achilles had gone too far in his grief, but no one, not even Ajax or Diomedes, had the courage to tell him to stop. As before, at the death of Patroclus, only Alex stepped forth to be the bearer of difficult news. Alex feared, as did all the others, that the one who dared to tell Achilles to stop would risk being killed by his sword and dragged himself around the pyre of Patroclus. Nevertheless, Alex approached. It was clear to him that the Accuser had seized hold of Achilles' heart and soul, and it was time that he, Alexander of Houston, the son of the Professor, faced the Accuser head on.

"Stacey," he said, placing his hands on his sister's shoulders, "I must enter the tent of Achilles. There is no other way. I must tell him to stop his grieving and return the body of Hector to his family. But there is something that you must do as well. You must find your way back to the Wall of Troy and enter the city through the secret passage shown us by Cassandra. Whatever it takes, you must get to King Priam. Tell him that he must fill a cart with gold and other costly treasures and bring it himself to the tent of Achilles. Perhaps with such a ransom, he can purchase back from Achilles the body of his son."

"But, Alex," said Stacey, "what if Achilles kills Priam as well?"

"I know, Stacey, I know. But we must take the risk. If I can convince Achilles to take pity on the father of his enemy, if I can get him to see his own father's pain in the suffering of Priam, then maybe, just maybe, we can break the hold of the Accuser. It's a small chance, Stacey, but it's our only one. Now run, run as fast as you can. If we wait any longer, I'm afraid I'll change my mind."

Stacey did not wait; she did not even pause. Like an arrow shot from the bow, she broke from Alex's side and ran without stopping to the wall. Stacey was fast, faster than most of the boys in her class, and in no time she found herself by the crack in the wall through which she and Alex had come a few days ago. Or was it a few months ago? It seemed to her that she had grown five years in those short days they had spent in the Greek camp.

Upon entering the city, she ran immediately to the chamber of Andromache. There she found her clutching Astyanax in her arms and weeping softly for her fallen husband. When she saw Stacey, she placed Astyanax gently on a pillow and hugged Stacey so hard that she feared she would break in two.

"Andromache," she said quietly, "please, you must take me at once to Priam. He must go alone into the Greek camp and bring back the body of Hector."

For a full minute longer, Andromache held Stacey closely. Then, she picked up Astyanax and, as the child slept in her arms, led Stacey to the throne room. There she found Priam and Hecuba kneeling at the altar, praying to the gods.

"King Priam," said Stacey, repeating Alex's words as best she could, "you must fill a cart with gold and other costly treasures and bring it yourself to the tent of Achilles. Perhaps with such a ransom, you can purchase back from Achilles the body of your son."

"Daughter," said Priam, "your words pierce me to the heart, and I have a mind to do as you say. If only I can gaze again on the body of my son, I shall accept whatever follows."

"No," cried out Hecuba, "you must not do this thing. Achilles will have no respect for you, but will kill you as you are. If only I could, I would tear the heart from Achilles and eat his liver raw. You must not go, my husband."

"Peace, Hecuba. We each have our lot in life and our duty to perform. Long ago, Zeus decided the day of my death. Why should I try to escape it? Let me rather seek to complete the task that has been given me. I shall do now as this child suggests. Please do not try to stop me."

Hecuba, accustomed as she was to pain and grief, said no more. As Priam set about gathering the gold for the ransom, she sat by the side of Andromache, and the women wept quietly together. Stacey too sat with them and shared in their tears.

Meanwhile, back in the Greek camp, her brother moved with slow and heavy steps toward the tent of Achilles. He reached out his hand and parted the curtain slightly so that a single beam of sunlight fell into the tent. There, sitting upright and motionless in the center, as if he were himself the wooden pole that held up the roof, was the son of Peleus. In his right arm, he clutched the ash spear, and with it, he traced lazy lines on the earth. As Alex stared at the mighty warrior, and as he sought vainly for the right words of comfort, his thoughts were carried back to one of the stories Daddy had told him as he had taken the children on their long tour of the Old Testament.

There was once a great King of Israel chosen by God to defeat his enemies and rule his people. His name was Saul, and he stood a head taller than any other man in Israel. For many years, he ruled justly and well, but when the time came for him to be tested, he sinned against the Lord and disobeyed his commandments. Grieved that he had ever chosen him as king, the Lord removed his protection from Saul, and an evil spirit began to torment the fallen king. For hours and days, he would sit brooding in his tent, and no one dared to come near him. Until one day, a boy, ruddy of face and strong in heart, came to the palace with his lyre in hand. Whenever the evil spirit fell upon Saul, the boy would sit beside him and play his lyre. He would sing sweetly of the love and mercy of God, and, as he sang, the heaviness would pass from Saul's chest and the evil spirit would depart. Of course, there were two times when Saul threw his spear at the boy and tried to pin him against the wall, but Alex tried not to think of that part of the story.

"Give me the courage of David," he prayed softly, and entered the tent. There on the ground he spied the lyre of Achilles and took it up in his hand. Sitting beside the warrior, Alex ran his fingers across the strings, and at once the air in the tent seemed to grow lighter. He prepared to strum the lyre a second time, but before he could, it was lifted out of his hands by a figure behind Achilles who until now had been hidden by the shadow of his back. It was Thetis. She smiled gently at Alex, and then she began to play the lyre as only a goddess of the sea could play it. The music grew sweeter and more insistent, and a deep groan sounded out from the chest of Achilles. He dropped his spear and rose to his feet. Another moment and he would have been out of the tent and on his way to the shore. But Alex bravely placed his body between Achilles and the curtain.

"No, Achilles, you shall not leave until I have spoken to you words that you must hear. I know that your grief for Patroclus is great, but the things you are doing are wrong. Achilles, you have lost your pity and your sense of shame. Stop it now, or you will lose your humanity as well."

Achilles looked at Alex with fierce anger in his eyes. With his right hand he reached for his sword and began to draw it slowly from its sheath. For a moment, Alex feared that Achilles had already lost his humanity, that it had been swallowed up by the Accuser and lost forever. But no, deep down in the eyes of the warrior, Alex saw a spark of that noble man he had first met, the one who had treated him and his sister with such warmth and hospitality. It was to that spark now that Alex addressed his words:

"Achilles, resist the Accuser, resist that voice inside your head that inflames your anger every time it starts to cool. The longer you refuse to eat and drink, the more you continue to defile Hector's body, the more you cut yourself off from the companionship of your friends, the more your grief and wrath will grow. This is not the proper way to grieve. The one who created us put in our hearts the strength to endure. We grieve for a time, and then the grief passes. But you, Achilles, are trapped in a cage that you yourself have made. Break that cage before it is too late. Cast off that voice that is separating you even now from yourself."

"Get out!" said Achilles, but the voice was not his own, "Leave this place and go back to your own world. What have I to do with you and your puny words? Achilles belongs to me now, and I alone shall tell him what to do. Soon Priam will be here, and then I shall direct your "noble" friend to drive his spear into the old man's heart. What do you care what happens in this tent. Achilles and Priam mean nothing to you. Mind your own business, boy, or I shall tell my slave to kill you as well."

"No," said Alex, addressing Achilles again and ignoring the taunts of the Accuser, "don't listen to him. He only wants to use you to keep the revenge and the killing going on forever. He hates you even more than you hate Hector. It's your nobleness and your goodness and your strength that he hates. He would crush every virtue within you and leave you nothing but an empty shell. Listen, Achilles, I told you before that there were four great virtues: justice and courage, wisdom and self-control. But these are not the only ones."

"Stop now, boy, I'm warning you!"

"My father told me once that the four virtues were the greatest things ever invented by man. But there are three more virtues, Achilles, virtues that your time and your culture know nothing about. They will be revealed later by God himself."

"Stop!" yelled Achilles, and his arm shot out and took a hold of Alex's throat. His fingers tightened, and Alex began to gasp for air. Black and red spots danced before his eyes, and he felt himself slowly slipping away.

"Alex!" cried Stacey, who had just reached the tent and pulled aside the curtain.

Surprised by the sudden sound and blinded for a second by the rays of sunlight that flooded into the tent, Achilles loosened his grip. Alex took a quick breath, and with all the strength he could muster, whispered the names of the three greater virtues:

"Faith... hope... love."

Achilles screamed as if a burning torch had been pressed to his chest, and released his grip on Alex's throat. Alex fell to his knees and rolled away from the center of the tent. Three times he breathed the air deep into his lungs, and the color returned to his face. Then, with new strength and determination, he walked over to the side of Achilles. In a voice filled with laughter and joy, he spoke winged words into the ear of the warrior:

"Faith, Achilles, is the first of the three, faith in all those things that you cannot see. Faith is a kind of trust that you hold hidden deep in your heart and that is strong and steady enough to stay true when all around you is shaken. Now you must have faith in the code of honor you were taught as a boy. You must have faith that the act of honor you perform today will be spoken of by future generations.

"And with that faith, you must combine hope. Only with hope can you see through the mist and fog of this war. You were made for a purpose, Achilles, and you must never lose sight of that purpose. You and Priam must now hope together for a future in which Greek and Trojan can live together as brothers and friends.

"But most of all, Achilles, you must learn love. Not that low love that Paris felt for Helen or Agamemnon felt for Chryseis or you, Achilles, felt for Briseis. Not even the higher love that Priam feels for Hecuba or that Hector felt for his people. I speak of a love that your world knows nothing about, but which it will someday learn. A love that allows you to move out of yourself toward another: to feel his pain, to share his sorrow, to even give your life for him. Achilles, this love you must now give to Priam. You must step outside of your anger and your pride and see things through the eyes of Hector's father."

Alex was going to say much more, to tell Achilles about a time when God himself would come down and live out these virtues on the earth, but before he could speak another word, the curtain parted again and Priam entered the tent. The moment he saw Achilles, Priam threw himself down at the feet of the warrior and took hold of his rough hands. Slowly, painfully, he pressed his lips to Achilles' hands and spoke:

"I beg of you, Achilles, accept the noble ransom I have brought you and return to me the body of my son. Look at me, Achilles, I could be Peleus, your own dear father. Have pity. I have done something that no man has ever done; I have kissed the hands of the man who killed my son."

Achilles gently pushed away the hands of Priam and crouched down beside him. With large tears he wept again the loss of his friend, while Priam, by his side, wept again the loss of his son. The sound of their weeping rose in the tent and fell again, like summer rain, to the ground. Then, when Achilles had finished his grieving, and the desire for it had left his mind and his body, he rose to his feet and extended his hand to Priam.

"Rise, noble king. Truly the heart within you is iron; else you would never have dared to come to my tent alone. But put your heart at ease. I shall return the body to you shortly, after my men have washed and prepared it with oil. You have nothing to fear from me.

Long years now I have thought on the horrors of death. In the past, I believed that since all men must someday die, we should spend our few short years in the endless quest for glory. Last week a different thought came into my mind: if we are all going to die, let us then live as long as we can. But when Patroclus was torn from me, I tossed that notion aside in favor of its opposite: if all of us must die, then let us do so quickly and be done with it. But now, Priam, my heart has learned a new lesson. If someday we all must die, then someday too we shall all lose someone who is most dear to us. And if that is the case, then the best we can do in this life is to grieve together."

"Yes," said Alex and Stacey together, "*that* is the proper way to grieve."

And then, because they had said the same thing at the same time, they both yelled out together:

"Jinx, personal jinx!"

Achilles stood still for a moment and stared at the two children. Then, wonder of wonders, he began to laugh. Alex and Stacey fell into each other's arms and laughed along with him till the whole tent echoed with the sound. But when they had had their fill of laughing, Achilles turned once again to Priam and addressed him with wise and gentle words:

"Priam, let us now call a truce for fourteen days. For the next two weeks, neither Greek nor Trojan shall take up spear or sword. Rather, we shall use our hands to collect our mutual dead and burn them with honor upon the funeral pyres. There have been grievous losses on both sides, and it is right and proper that we should mourn them fully… and together."

The next few minutes were a flurry of activity as Priam wheeled in the ransom and spread it out before the glowing eyes of Achilles. Next, the body of Hector was itself wheeled in on a new cart. The hair and face and hands of the fallen warrior had been carefully groomed, and he was dressed in a costly robe laced with silver and gold. Priam took the body of his son into his arms and spoke to it tender words of regret. Then, with the encouragement of Achilles, Priam attached the cart to two oxen and drove them on toward the wall. As Hector entered again into the city he loved, the three women who were closest to his heart—Hecuba, Andromache, and Helen—led the lament from the top of the watchtower. For nine days, the Trojans mourned the passing of their most noble warrior, but on the tenth, they committed his body to the flames.

And thus they buried Hector, son of Priam and the Prince of all Troy.

The Fall of Troy

As Priam carried off the body of his son, Achilles himself left the tent to visit once more the funeral pyre of Patroclus. The children remained behind with Thetis, and the three of them together stared at the wonderful engravings on the shield of Achilles.

"Yes, children," said Thetis, "I know what you are thinking, and I agree with you. Achilles has made the right choice. He has chosen the city of life. But come, there is someone who longs to speak with you, and you must not make him wait."

As Alex and Stacey looked on, Thetis waved her hand around a spot in the floor that seemed lower than the ground beside it. As she did, the spot began to swirl and sunk even further into the earth. Thetis then brought her hands together in a loud clap that shook the sides of the tent. Immediately, dirt and sand flew everywhere, and for several seconds, neither Alex nor Stacey could see anything. But when the dust settled, and they looked again at the spot on the ground, they found to their amazement a deep hole with steps leading down.

"Children, no words of mine could thank you enough for what you have done for my son. Instead, let me give you each a present to remember me by. For you, Alex, I give this corral ring. Inside of it, you will find a vial of liquid taken from a plant that grows only on the very bottom of the ocean. The liquid has magical properties and can counteract the effect of any drug or poison known to man. For you, Stacey, I give this silver necklace from which hangs a pearl of strange and mystical powers. Rub it in your hand, and it will glow with the light of a hundred candles. Swallow it, and it will allow you to breathe underwater like a fish for thirty minutes. But beware, only swallow it if your situation is dire, for once swallowed it will dissolve away in your throat. Now go, children. Follow the steps, and you will be safe. May the gods of Olympus smile down on you and bless you as you have blessed me."

The pathway was steep and it was almost pitch black in the hole, but Stacey rubbed her pearl and the passage was immediately illuminated by the glow of a hundred candles. Alex and Stacey followed the glow and found, to their great surprise, that it led them back to the river that ran under the palace of Priam. And there, on the other side of the river, they saw Pan. They were both so excited that they ran right through the water and gave him a warm double hug.

"Well done!" said Pan in a voice that stirred the waters, "You have both shown yourselves faithful in the task that was given you. Because of you two and the courage you have shown, your whole civilization has been saved."

"Do you mean," said Alex, "that we have stopped the war and that now Achilles won't die and Troy will not be destroyed?"

"No, my son," said Pan sadly, "after the fourteen-day truce has ended, the war will begin again and Achilles will be killed by an arrow from the bow of Paris. Many more soldiers will perish on the field of battle until, in the tenth year of the war, Odysseus will devise a plan for breaking through the Wall of Troy.

"The Greeks will build a giant horse of wood but will leave it hollow inside. They will wheel the horse in front of the Wall of Troy and then pretend to board their ships and sail back to Greece. In their ignorance and folly, the Trojans, refusing to heed the warnings of Cassandra, will take the horse into their city and celebrate wildly the end of the war. But while they sleep, a trap door will open in the bottom of the wooden horse, and the Greek soldiers who had been hiding within will climb out and open wide the Scaean Gates. By that time the Greeks will have returned from their ships and will be waiting outside the walls. Like a raging fire they will fan out through the city killing and destroying all that they see. All the men, even Priam himself, they will put to the sword, and the women—Hecuba, Andromache, Cassandra, all of them—they will drag away to Greece to be slaves."

"But what about Astyanax?" asked Stacey.

"Alas, my child, he too will perish, thrown to his death from the watchtower."

"Then all is lost," said Alex, "We have failed and the Accuser has won."

"Failed! Failed? You haven't failed. You have won! When Homer puts together his great epic, he will not end it with the fall of Troy and the death of Astyanax. No, children, he will end it here, with Achilles' return of the body of Hector and the truce to bury their dead. Not with destruction but on a final note of hope, peace, and reconciliation shall Homer bring his heroic tale to a close."

"I understand," said Stacey, "Daddy told us that Homer did not begin the *Iliad* in the beginning but in the middle. Now you are telling us he won't end it at the ending, but in the middle too."

"Yes, exactly. You are both thinking that because Troy will fall that the Accuser has won, but he has not. When you convinced Achilles, like Hercules, to reject the evil of the Accuser and choose the path of virtue, you helped to turn a corner that will lead not to death but to civilization.

"In the end, there is only one way to defeat the Accuser, a difficult and dangerous way that you both have witnessed. You must lure him, clever serpent that he is, out of hiding, make him think that the victory soon will be his. Of course, in drawing him out, you risk, like Achilles, being struck in the heel; but only at the moment that he strikes your heel will you be given the chance to crush his head. That is how it always works, children: life snatched back out of the jaws of death, victory out of defeat, goodness that triumphs out of the heart of evil."

"Just like my name," said Stacey.

"Your name?" asked Pan.

"Yes, my name, my *full* name is Anastasia. And Daddy told us once that Anastasia means resurrection, life out of death."

"And that is exactly what you two have helped to accomplish. For do not be fooled: Achilles *was* dead, lost to men and to the gods, but you helped to draw him back into the land of the living. If even Achilles can put aside his wrath and take pity on Priam, then civilization is possible. It is a small beginning, but it *is* a beginning. Henceforth, nothing will be the same."

"So does that mean we can go home, now?" said Stacey.

"Not yet, little one. There is still work to be done. You have helped to set back in place the code of honor by which soldiers fight and enemies are treated, but these are not enough. For a civilization to survive, it must also cultivate the arts and the virtues of peace. You have helped show Achilles, and through him the world, that civilization and the choices that go with it are possible; you must now help a second hero to discover *why* such a thing is worth fighting for. It is time to leave the battlefield and enter the world of the family, of fathers and sons, husbands and wives. You caught a glimpse of this already in the final meeting of Hector and Andromache, but there such things were overshadowed by the war."

"What must we do, Pan?" asked Alex.

"You must help Odysseus to return to his island home of Ithaca and to be reunited with his wife, Penelope (pe NELL oh pee), and his son, Telemachus (te LEM a kus). When the Greeks defeat Troy, they will turn barbaric, and the gods will punish them for their cruelty. For many, like Agamemnon, their homecoming will be a bitter one; for others, like Odysseus, the road home will be long and fraught with danger. You must help the family of Odysseus to find each other again, to rediscover for themselves and the generations to come the true nature of the good life. Are you ready to take up this challenge?"

"I am," said Alex,

"So am I," said Stacey.

"Good, then let us return now to the deck, where I shall take you ahead many months and place you on board the ship of Odysseus. And as we fly, Alex, I would very much like to hear more of this higher love. I have many questions to ask you."

— Part —

3

Fathers and Sons

*"If there were
some token now, some mark to make the division
clear between friend and friend, the true and the false!"*
—Euripides

Longing for Home

Ask the average person what word first comes into his mind when he hears the name "Odysseus," and he will most likely say "wanderer." Odysseus did, after all, spend long years sailing from one strange island to the next, where he met all manner of friendly islanders, man-eating monsters, and exotic women. Still, it is not really fair to speak of Odysseus as one driven by a wanderlust to travel the far reaches of the seven seas. Despite his journeys and his many adventures, the Odysseus of Homer has really only one desire in his heart: to go home.

Indeed, when the beautiful nymph, Calypso, offered to make Odysseus immortal if he would only forget his wife and his home and remain with her forever on her island, he answered her gently that he could not accept her gift. And when she asked him how he could chose a mortal woman who would soon grow old and weak over her, an immortal goddess, he said in reply: "Lady, all that you say is true, for my poor Penelope cannot hope to match you in beauty or form or skill. Nevertheless, I must return to her and to Ithaca. It is the one thing that I long for. Without her I am not myself. I must go home."

That is how he felt in the ninth year of his journey home, and it was also how he felt when he first began his odyssey on the morning after the fall of Troy. As he set off in the lead ship, followed closely by five other ships filled with the finest sailors of Ithaca, he thought longingly of the arms of Penelope and of meeting his only child, who had been but a mere infant when he had left for Troy ten long years before. The Aegean stretched out before him like a blue sky on a cloudless day, and his sails blossomed in the wind like a field of lilies.

In hopes of gaining extra supplies for his men, Odysseus soon ran ashore on the island of Ismarus, where his men, accustomed to long years of fighting, quickly sacked the town and plundered its stores of food and wine. Overjoyed by their success, the men spread out on the beach and feasted themselves for the rest of the day. Odysseus encouraged them to finish their feast and board the ships immediately, but the men continued in their folly to eat and drink. And as they fed their bellies, oblivious to all danger, the inhabitants of the island regrouped and attacked them on the beach. They barely escaped with their lives, leaving behind on the sand the dead bodies of six men from each ship.

The violence of their actions must have influenced somehow the winds, for the moment their ships left shore a storm rose and carried them far away into waters uncharted on any map. For seven days, they sailed blind, tossed by the wind like so many toy boats. Odysseus, eager to get his ships back on course, slept not a wink, but on the eighth day, exhaustion overtook him, and he fell into a deep slumber. Many hours later, as the moon was reaching its zenith, he was awakened by a strange whirring sound that seemed to be coming from high above the ship. He was never able to identify the source of the whirring, but when he rose and walked onto the deck, he was greeted by the sight of two children who looked to him to be just a bit seasick.

"Are you not the two children that I saw lurking in the tent of Achilles?"

"We are, Odysseus. My name is Alex, and this is my sister, Stacey. We have been sent by the great goddess Athena to aid you in your journey home. May we have your permission to come aboard, sir?"

"Permission granted! I must say that I do not always understand the ways of Athena, but it is always the best policy to accept her gifts. You two shall stay with me in my cabin, and when we arrive at Ithaca, you, Alex, will be given a suit of armor and a sword of the finest bronze, and your sister shall be given pearl earrings and a necklace of pure gold."

"I would like that," said Stacey.

"Very well, then, it is settled. But come now, it is time for you to eat and sleep. I feel in my bones that tomorrow we will strike land."

Odysseus, as it turned out, was right in his prediction. The next day they came to an island of rare beauty. Flowers of every color grew in plenty, and pools of crystal clear water dotted the landscape. The trees hung heavy with fruit, and there seemed to be a bird of paradise perched on every tree. The natives were as beautiful and gentle as their island and seemed to walk from place to place in a sort of trance. They took the sailors by the hand and led them to the top of a hill. There they brought for them to eat a strange type of fruit that none of them had ever seen before. The natives called it lotus, and it had a sweet and lazy taste that made one think of a long summer day.

Alex and Stacey, who were a bit suspicious of these overly-friendly natives climbed to the top of a tree and looked down on the men as they fed hungrily on the honey-sweet lotus. Odysseus himself ate of the fruit, and as the children watched him, they noticed a mysterious change come over his face. Where his eyes had before seemed alert, ever straining ahead, they now seemed to droop and to turn inward. The other men, too, lost the determination and the strength that had once shone in their eyes and took on the look of men who live in a dream. Sensing danger, Alex and Stacey climbed down and rushed over to the side of Odysseus.

"Come on, Odysseus," said Alex, shaking him by his shoulders, "I think that we should leave this place right away."

"Why should we leave?" said Odysseus, and his voice sounded dreamy and far away, "It is so nice here, and the lotus is so sweet."

"But your wife and your son, Penelope and Telemachus. They are waiting to see you. You must get your men back on the ship and sail home to Ithaca."

"Home… home… why do you speak to me of home? This island is my home. I don't know anyone named Penelope or any place called Ithaca. I've always lived here. But now leave me alone. I am very tired and would like to sleep some more on this warm hillside."

"No, Odysseus, no!" shouted Alex, "This is not your home; it's a trap, a false Ithaca. You have to *remember*, Odysseus. You can't forget who you are."

"No, no, go away little boy. I don't know anyone named Odysseus. I just want to lie here and feed on the lotus."

"What shall we do, Alex?" said Stacey, "What shall we do? He's forgotten *everything*, and so has everyone else I'm afraid. This lotus must be like a drug that makes you forget."

"Of course, Stacey, that's it. The lotus *is* a drug, and if it is, then the ring that Thetis gave me should counteract it. Come on, prop up Odysseus' head and help me to get a drop of this liquid into his mouth."

Stacey did so, and the moment the liquid touched his tongue, Odysseus leapt to his feet, and his eyes filled with their old fire.

"Thank you, children. You have saved me from a terrible fate. When I set out from Troy, I thought that the only thing that could stop me from returning to Ithaca would be storms and enemies and other threats to my body. But now I see that there is another danger I must be wary of: the danger of accepting a false homecoming. To think I had almost abandoned Penelope and Ithaca and my own dear son to live like an ignorant savage on this island. To think that a man who killed a hundred Trojans in battle should almost be conquered by a handful of fruit. The very thought stirs my blood! But come, you must help me to drag these other poor fools back on to the ships. We must leave this place without delay."

Alex and Stacey did as they had been ordered, but it was no easy task. The men cried and groaned and held on to the lotus as though it were more precious than gold, as though they would sell their very families to have another taste. It was a pathetic sight indeed, but with the help of Odysseus, they eventually forced all the men back on to the ships. Luckily the lotus had made them as weak as they were forgetful. As for the lotus-eaters themselves, they neither fought to keep a hold of their new found "friends" nor even bothered to wave goodbye as the ships sailed away. They merely continued to eat their lotus and to stretch out lazily on the warm hillside.

Odysseus, glad to be off the island, opened full the sails, and the ships glided swiftly o'er the wine-dark sea. On the third day, they ran ashore on the island of the Cyclopes, fierce giants with a single eye in the middle of their foreheads who neither sail the sea themselves nor care much for those who do. Their island is a magical one and gives forth its fruits, its grains, and its vegetables without need of farmers to sow or reap it. They lived an easy life on their land of plenty, and it was perhaps for this reason that they never learned to work together or to form a society. No assemblies ever met on the island of the Cyclopes, but each lived in his own cave and ignored his neighbors completely. They knew nothing of civilization and cared nothing for its laws and its virtues.

They did not know, or care, that the great father of the gods, Zeus of the thunderbolt, held sacred the relationship between guest and host, and that certain duties were expected of each. To be a good host you were to take into your house any stranger who came to your door in need. You were to feed him first and only then ask his name and his origin. As for the guest, he was to take only what was given him as a gift, and he was never to stay longer than he was welcome. As long as these laws were upheld, civilization was possible, and sailors could travel safely from one port to the next. But take them away or break them, as Paris did when he stole Helen, and only disaster could follow.

Unfortunately, Odysseus knew nothing of the Cyclopes when he landed on their peaceful shore. Thinking all was safe, he left the ship and, with Alex, Stacey and a dozen of his best men by his side, set out to explore the island. In the event that he might meet some friendly natives, he brought with him a special gift: a blood-red wine so strong that those who drank of it would first mix it with ten cups of water.

Gift in hand, Odysseus and his men soon discovered an enormous cave filled with buckets swimming in goat's milk and baskets stuffed with cheese. The furniture in the cave looked like furniture you might find anywhere else, except for the fact that it was three sizes bigger and was very rough to the touch. As there was no one home and the men were very hungry, they immediately began to gorge themselves on the milk and the cheese. When they had finished, and they had taken another look at the giant furniture, they all turned to Odysseus at once and advised him to return to the ship. None of them particularly cared to meet the owner of the cave, especially after they had helped themselves to so much of his food.

"No," said Odysseus, "let us wait a little longer. I would like to meet the owner. Perhaps he will give us gifts to take back to our ships."

Though Alex and Stacey said nothing, it was fast becoming clear to them that Odysseus and his men were not only acting like bad guests but like fools as well. What they did not realize was that these bad guests were about to meet a host who was far, far worse.

— Chapter —

18

In the Cave of the Cyclops

The owner of the cave was named Polyphemus (pa lee FEE mus), and he was, by trade, a herder of goats. He hated strangers even more than his neighbors did and kept to himself at all times. Each morning he would drive his sheep and goats to pasture, feeding them on the grassy hills that lay in abundance near his cave. He lived on meat and cheese and drank only water and milk. He had never seen a grape in his life and had never tasted wine. He was a very suspicious sort of person and so while he slept or was away from his cave, he would cover up the entrance with a huge round stone that fifty men with ropes and carts would have a hard time budging from its place. Today, however, he had been in such a rush to get to pasture that he had forgotten to roll the stone back into place.

The sun was just setting in the west when Polyphemus drove his goats back into the cave. As he entered, his nose caught the scent of something strange, and he quickly reached back with his arms and rolled the stone in front of the entrance. Then, in a voice that echoed off the walls like a great waterfall, he spoke:

"Strangers! Who are you and why have you come to my cave? Are you pirates who have come to plunder my goods? Show yourselves. I know you are there."

Odysseus stepped forward and spoke out in a soothing voice: "Cyclops, we are not pirates come to plunder you, but poor sailors whose ship was dashed against your shore by a storm. We have come in hopes that you will heed the laws of Zeus and show us hospitality."

"Fool," thundered the Cyclops, "What have I to do with Zeus and his thunderbolts? They do not scare me."

And with that, he reached out his hand and scooped up two of Odysseus' sailors as if they had been rag dolls. With a quick flick of his wrist, he dashed their heads against the wall of the cave with such force and speed that their skulls cracked open, and their brains spilled out on the floor. Then, as Odysseus and his men lifted their hands in prayer to Zeus, Polyphemus tore the two sailors limb from limb and ate them raw. When he had finished, there was nothing left of them: skin, hair, bones, and all had disappeared into the cruel mouth of the Cyclops.

"Evil man," said Odysseus, "is this how you treat your guests?"

But the Cyclops ignored him. With another flick of his wrist, he emptied an entire bucket of milk down his throat. Then, without another word, he stretched himself out on the floor of the cave and went to sleep. Odysseus walked over to the side of the sleeping giant, pulled out his sword, and prepared to plunge it into his heart. But before he could, Alex ran up behind him and grabbed his arm.

"Are you crazy, Odysseus?" he said, "If you kill the Cyclops, we will never get out of this cave. There is no way we could move that stone by ourselves. We would be trapped in here forever."

"You speak wisely. In my rashness I almost doomed us all. Let us search this cave and see if there is not another way out. If only we had a torch!"

"We don't need a torch," said Stacey, "I have all the light we need right here."

With a flick of *her* wrist, Stacey rubbed her pearl, and the cave immediately filled with a soft glow. She took off the necklace and handed it to Odysseus, who held it out in front of him and began to walk slowly around the edge of the cave. To his great dismay, he could find no other exit, but he did discover, in the very back, an old walking stick that the Cyclops must have tossed aside. It was well over ten feet long and was made of strong wood. "Yes," he murmured to himself, "it could work." Then, speaking aloud:

"Men, get out your swords and sharpen the end of this stick. Make sure the point is long and narrow. When you are done, hide the stick so that the Cyclops will not see it. When you are done, lay down and get as much sleep as you can. Tomorrow, you will need all your strength."

Though no one really believed they could fight off the Cyclops with a stick, no matter how sharp and long it was, they obeyed Odysseus. They did a fine job with their swords, but when it came to sleeping, I'm afraid none of them were very successful.

Polyphemus rose early the next morning and milked his goats. As the milk splashed in the pails, he removed a large piece of cheese from a nearby basket and devoured it in one bite. Then, without saying a word, he scooped up two more of Odysseus' men and dashed their heads against the wall. What was good enough for dinner, it seemed, was good enough for breakfast.

"O Cyclops," said Odysseus when the monster had finished his horrible meal, "wouldn't you like something strong to wash down that man flesh with? I have something here that is far tastier than your milk."

Polyphemus strode over to Odysseus and held out his hand. With a smile on his face and a twinkle in his eye, Odysseus poured some of the wine he had brought with him into a cup and handed it to the Cyclops. He drank it down in a single gulp.

"This is very good, human. If you will tell me your name and give me more of that drink, I shall give you a special gift."

"I thank you, Cyclops. My name is … Nobody. But here, have another drink."

Polyphemus took the second cup offered to him and gulped it down more quickly than the first. Seven times Odysseus filled the cup; seven times the Cyclops drank it down. But when he went to pour the eighth, he noticed that the giant was moving unsteadily and that his single eye seemed glazed and drowsy.

"Very well, Nobody," said Polyphemus, who was by now so drunk that he could barely stand up, "Here is the gift I promised you. I was going to eat you for dinner tonight, but now instead, I shall eat you last after all your other men. That is my gift to you."

And then, having had his nasty say, he collapsed on to the floor. His head rolled to one side, his mouth opened up, and the contents of his stomach poured out, including, as you might guess, the mangled body parts of Odysseus' men.

"Ugh," though Stacey, "What do we do now?"

As if he had read her thoughts, Odysseus ran to the back of the cave and took up the stick that his men had sharpened the night before. With the help of six of his strongest sailors, he lifted high the stick and drove it full force into the single eye of the Cyclops. Polyphemus cried out in pain and jumped to his feet. With his right hand, he pulled the stick from his eye and threw it in front of him. In a loud voice that shook the cave, he yelled:

"Friends and neighbors, come help me, there is an evil man in my cave who has put out my eye."

"What are you saying, Polyphemus?" said a voice from outside the cave, "Who has put out your eye?"

"Nobody has put out my eye. Nobody has done it."

"C'mon," said a group of voices all at once, "Polyphemus has lost his mind. In any case, that's the first time I've heard him speak in three years."

"Friends, you must help me catch Nobody and punish him," screamed Polyphemus, but by then his neighbors had already left to tend their flocks. Odysseus laughed gently to himself that the foolish Cyclops had fallen for his trick.

When he realized that no one was coming to help him, Polyphemus began groping around the cave with his hands, hoping to catch Odysseus or one of his men. But they were too fast for him. Soon, the cave filled with the sound of bleating goats and sheep eager to climb the hills and have their breakfast. Polyphemus, who loved his flock even if he was an evil cannibal, couldn't bear to hear them bleating in hunger and rolled the stone away from the entrance. For the men who had blinded him, however, he felt no such compassion.

Knowing that the men would surely try to escape now that the stone had been rolled away, Polyphemus crouched down on the tips of his toes and pressed his back against the entrance to the cave. Then, as if he were the catcher in a baseball game, he held open his hands in hopes of catching the men as they tried to run through his legs.

But once again, Odysseus was too smart for him. With some rope he found in the cave, he tied together the sheep and goats in groups of three across. Under the belly of each of the middle sheep, he tied up tightly one of his men. The trick worked perfectly. As the sheep trotted out of the cave, the blind giant felt the tops of their heads and let them go safely. As for Odysseus himself, he chose a single large ram and gripped on to its fleece with his bare hands. This ram, as it turned out, was the leader of the flock and the personal favorite of Polyphemus. Usually it was the first one out of the cave, but today, weighed down by the heavy body of Odysseus, it was the last of the flock to go out to pasture.

"Oh my ram," said Polyphemus after he had felt his head and recognized which it was, "always you are the first to leave, but today you linger behind. Is it because you feel pity for your poor master who has been blinded by a puny human? If only you could talk, ram, I know you would tell me where Nobody is hiding."

Luckily for Odysseus, who was hanging on to the ram's belly with all his might, the dumb creature did not speak. Instead, he carried the crafty sea captain out of the cave where he joined up with his men and ran full speed to the ship. In no time at all, the ships weighed their anchors and put out to sea. But alas, Odysseus in his pride and folly could not help but taunt the Cyclops whom he had so cleverly defeated.

"Cyclops!" he yelled, as his ship pulled away from the shore, "If anyone asks you who put out your eye, you can tell him that it was city-sacking Odysseus, King of Ithaca."

It was a foolish thing to do, but Odysseus could not resist the temptation to brag a bit over his victory. In response, Polyphemus, who had found his way to the beach, lifted a large stone and hurled it in the direction of Odysseus' voice. The stone hit the water just in front of the ship and created a wave that pushed the ship back to the beach. Terrified of being caught again by the Cyclops, the men rushed to the oars and rowed with all their might.

"Alas," cried the Cyclops, "it had been prophesied to me that a man named Odysseus would one day put out my eye, but I had always thought this Odysseus would be a giant or a god, not some weak little human."

"I only wish I could have taken your life as well as your eye," shouted Odysseus.

Again, the Cyclops lifted a boulder, this one half the size of the ship itself, and hurled it toward the source of the voice. Again, it hit the water and washed the ship back toward the shore. Frantically, the men took to the oars once more and rowed the ship back out to sea. Odysseus looked like he was going to speak again, but the children rushed over to him and begged him to stop. He agreed this time to keep silent, but the damage had already been done. What no one on the ship knew, least of all Odysseus, was that Polyphemus was none other than the son of Poseidon, brother to Zeus and the Lord of the Sea.

"Father," cried Polyphemus, as the ship sailed away, "the sea is yours and all that is in it. If you are truly my father, then hear my prayer. Prevent this Odysseus from ever seeing Ithaca again, or, if you cannot prevent his return, then make his homecoming a bitter one. Let him come home tired and worn after years of wandering, and let him find his home in ruins, overcome by evil guests like the ones he brought with him to steal from my cave. Let him pay dearly for his wicked deeds. Do not fail me, Poseidon."

"Alex," said Stacey, "I thought that you had defeated the Accuser. But now it sounds like he has returned."

"I know, Stacey. I'm afraid that Odysseus may have woken him up with his prideful words. It looks like we're in for another adventure."

The Curse Begins to Fall

The next few days of sailing were calm ones, and Alex and Stacey began to hope that their fears might be mistaken. Morale on the ships was high, and Odysseus seemed to have learned his lesson and was decidedly more humble than before. The children enjoyed walking on the deck of the ship, and Stacey even ventured a climb up to the crow's-nest. From there, she could see for miles and miles around the ship. The view was breathtaking. She even hoped that she herself might be the one to catch sight of the next island. Indeed, for a second, she thought she did see an island, but when she blinked her eyes, it was gone. Five minutes later, she saw it again, but before she could shout, "Land ho," the island vanished. Three more times the island appeared, only to disappear a few seconds later. Finally, it dawned on her what was happening. What she was seeing, wonder of wonders, was a floating island, one that moved on the sea as though it were a ship or a great turtle.

"Land ho" she cried, and climbed down the mast to tell Odysseus what she had seen. His heart leaped up when he heard the news, and he swore he would track down the island if it took him all week. As it turned out, it only took two hours to locate the island and dock his ships on it. The moment they landed, six young men and six young women who looked like gods in their strength and beauty came to meet them at the shore and took them to their home to eat. They were the sons and daughters of none other than Aeolus (AY oh lus), the god of the wind. Aeolus had given his daughters to his sons in marriage (gods do things like that), and, together with his own wife, the fourteen of them lived together in a single house with a courtyard as large and as lovely as the one in the palace of Priam. All day long they did nothing but sing and play, and in the afternoons and the evenings, they feasted on meat and wine and the finest fruits and vegetables. At night they slept on beds like clouds, each beside his loving wife. When Odysseus' men arrived, they were in the process of cooking three lambs and a small calf over an open fire. The smell made Alex and Stacey think of a Texas barbecue, and they both got a little homesick.

After the feast, Aeolus asked Odysseus his name and his story, and everyone listened in silence as Odysseus spoke of the Trojan War and of the terrors of the Cyclops' cave. But when he had finished, and, one by one, the sons and daughters of the wind retired for the night, Aeolus took Odysseus aside and gave him a special gift meant for his eyes alone.

"In this golden bag tied with a golden cord," he said, "I have locked up all the winds that could blow you off course. As long as you keep this locked away in your ship, no ill breeze shall harm you, and your ships will sail straight for Ithaca. On the eighth morning of your departure, you shall arrive safely home."

Odysseus was overjoyed and could barely sleep the entire night. When morning came, he boarded his men on the ships and hoisted the sails. Such was his excitement, he did not eat or sleep for seven days, but stood always at the prow of the ship making sure she stayed on course. As the sun began to set on the seventh day, Odysseus looked forth from the ship and saw the stony crags of his native Ithaca. He was so close that he could see the watch fires lit on the tops of the crags and people driving their goats back home. Relieved that he had made it safely, he lay on his bed and took a well-deserved rest.

If only he had not done so! While he slept, the men on his ship who had seen the golden bag but did not know what was inside it began to murmur amongst themselves.

"I'll bet there is gold in that bag, but Odysseus does not want to share it with us."

"Of course, why else would he hide it in the bottom of the ship?"

"Just like Aeolus to give the captain something and forget about us."

Alex who couldn't sleep and was walking on the deck to get some fresh air overheard the men talking and tried to reason with them:

"What are you saying? Odysseus is your captain. Hasn't he always treated you fairly? If there is gold in that bag, I'm sure he will give you your fair share."

But the men refused to listen to him and pushed him out of their cabin. "This is the Accuser's work," Alex thought to himself,

"Stirring up suspicion and resentment is just the kind of thing he would do."

But whether it was the Accuser or the curse of Polyphemus or the men's own greed and folly, the outcome was the same. The moment the wicked sailors grabbed a hold of the golden bag and removed the golden cord a hundred winds rushed out and the ships were blown off course. Odysseus woke up just in time to see the watch fires of Ithaca receding away behind him. For seven days the winds blew wildly, and several of the best sailors were blown overboard to their deaths. In the end, the ships were driven back to the floating island of Aeolus, but this time, when Odysseus came on shore, he found no friendly welcome.

"Leave this island and never return," said Aeolus, "It is clear to me you are cursed by the gods; such a thing could only happen to a man who had committed some terrible crime."

With heavy hearts, Odysseus and his men left the island and sailed blindly through strange waters and beneath strange stars. After many weeks, they came upon a land where the sun shone for twenty hours a day and where a laborer could work a double shift and still not see darkness. The island had a natural harbor surrounded on three sides by steep cliffs. The other five ships in Odysseus' fleet drove straight into the harbor, but Odysseus, who had grown more cautious with each adventure, docked his ship just outside the harbor. If only his men had done the same, for here too there lived a race of giant cannibals known as the Laestrygonians (less tri GO nee ens). With promises of hospitality, the men were lured to the palace of the King, where they were immediately set upon by guards. The Queen herself ate three men before the sailors could rush back to their ship.

And then it was that they wished they had docked their ships alongside that of Odysseus. As they frantically tried to steer their ships out of the harbor, the Laestrygonians threw rocks down upon them, tearing their sails and smashing their masts. Then, as if they were boys pulling tasty morsels of meat out of a crockpot with long forks, the Laestrygonians sat on the crags and stabbed long spears down onto the decks of the ships. With each stab, they skewered a sailor and pulled him upward to be eaten alive. Odysseus and the men on his ship watched with horror, but there was nothing they could do. In less than an hour, the other five ships had been destroyed and their crews either eaten or drowned.

Cursing his fate and the folly that had led him to taunt the Cyclops, Odysseus turned his prow toward evening and slipped away into the growing darkness.

An Enchantress and a Prophet

It was many days before anyone on Odysseus' ship spoke a single word. Alex and Stacey stayed below deck for most of the time, afraid to sleep lest nightmares of the giant Laestrygonians should visit them. No one, not even Odysseus, had any idea where they were or where they were headed. They just kept sailing. On the fourteenth day, the man in the crow's-nest spotted a small island, and Odysseus, badly in need of supplies and fresh water, decided to make landfall. Once on the beach, he set up a makeshift camp and sent out a group to explore the island. The group didn't particularly like their job, but they obeyed Odysseus and set out immediately. Alex and Stacey, who had grown more and more suspicious of the sailors since the time they had opened the golden bag, followed quietly behind. It seemed to them that the best way they could help Odysseus was to keep a close eye on his men.

Much of the island was covered with thick trees, and it was hard going for about an hour. But when at last they had broken through the thickest part of the forest, they found, to their surprise, a small but brightly colored cottage tucked away in a clearing. Lazy clouds of smoke rose up from the chimney, and the sound of a woman singing filled the air. All around the cottage were a series of pens that held various kinds of animals: lions, bears, wolves, pigs, dogs, and many more. The men approached the cottage and found to their surprise that even the most fierce-looking of the animals seemed as harmless and gentle as rabbits. The wolves, the pigs, and even the lions walked up to the men and rubbed against them with their rough hides and their moist noses. Alex and Stacey, who had learned by now to be careful and not to rush into anything, stayed behind in the forest and watched the men from a distance.

As they watched, the lady of the house, who had been singing so sweetly, came out and greeted the men. She hugged each of them warmly and sat them at her table. Then she brought out to them platters covered with food and goblets brimming over with wine. But after each of them had taken a deep drink from his goblet, the lady rushed in between them, removed a silver wand from her cloak, and touched each of their heads in succession. When she did this, all the men fell down on their hands and knees and began to cry out in pain. Their faces grew soft like clay, and their ears and their noses began to change shape. Their clothes fell away, and hair sprang out on every inch of their bodies. Their hands grew hard and bony; their legs were swallowed up by their knees and grew as hard and bony as their hands.

Alex and Stacey turned their eyes away for a moment, and when they looked again, they saw not men but a group of pigs where the sailors had been. The woman opened one of the pens and herded the pigs inside. They squealed terribly and their eyes filled with tears, but the woman paid no heed to their cries. She merely threw them some nuts and pods and then went back into the cottage.

Neither Alex nor Stacey stayed to see any more. As fast as their legs could carry them, they ran back to Odysseus and told him the whole story.

"I have heard of such enchantments," said Odysseus, "but I never thought I would experience one firsthand. Such witches must be handled with great care and cunning."

"Odysseus," said Alex, "I think I know what you can do. Do you remember the liquid we gave you to counteract the effects of the lotus? I still have several more drops left in my ring. Perhaps if you put a few drops in the goblet when the witch is not looking, the power of her spell will be broken. Then, when she touches you with her wand, you can grab a hold of her throat and make her swear by the river Styx that she will not harm you or your men."

"You know," said Stacey, "the lady did not look that evil to me. I think that she is just lonely. Maybe if you are kind to her after you steal her wand, she will give you a kiss and invite you to stay with her."

"C'mon, Stacey, she's a witch. Didn't you see what she did to those men?"

"I don't care, Alex. I still think she looks nice."

"Alright, children," said Odysseus with a laugh, "I think both of your ideas are good ones. Let me have your ring now, Alex, and I will see if we can't catch this witch at her own game."

After leaving a few men behind to keep watch on the ship, Odysseus gathered the rest of his crew—the ones that were still human that is!—and had them follow him into the woods. When they had reached the clearing, Odysseus ordered Alex, Stacey, and his men to stay behind in the woods while he went on to the cottage. If he were successful, he would call out to them, but if he were not, he told them that they must return to the ship and sail away.

As Odysseus approached the cottage, the animals that were not penned up came over to him and licked his hand. The pigs that had once been his men all began squealing at once as if they were trying to warn him of the danger to come. But Odysseus kept his eyes forward and walked straight to the door of the cottage. Before he could reach it, the lady of the house glided out in her white robe and gave the brave captain a warm hug. Then, as she had done before, she invited him to sit down and laid before him tasty food and sparkling wine. Odysseus asked her if she could also bring him some olive oil, and, as she did, he opened Alex's ring and poured the rest of the liquid into the cup of wine she had given him. When she returned with the oil, he spoke to her in a merry tone of voice as if the two had been old friends. She watched him carefully to see if he would drink the wine, and, when she saw that he had drained the cup completely, she pulled out her wand and touched it to his head.

To her great surprise, Odysseus did not fall to his knees and cry out in pain. Rather, he leapt up to his feet and grabbed her by the throat so as to prevent her from speaking any spells. Seizing her wand and dashing it to the ground, Odysseus looked the witch straight in her eyes and told her that unless she swore by Styx not to use any further magic against him or his crew that he would stran-gle her. The witch nodded her head, and when Odysseus loosened his grip, she made the oath as she had been told.

When she had finished, Odysseus, remembering Stacey's advice, let go of her throat and gave her back her wand. Then he took her hand in his and spoke to her winning words:

"Fair goddess, forgive my rough treatment of you, but I had to make sure you would not cause further harm to my crew. But now that you have sworn the oath, I can see that you are by far the loveli-est woman I have met in all of my travels. Your eyes sparkle like the stars on a cloudless night, and your hair is more golden than the noon-day sun."

The lady smiled and offered her ruby lips to be kissed by the handsome stranger. Then with a voice that sang more than it spoke, she said:

"O wanderer of the sea, my name is Circe (SIR see), and I am the daughter of the sun. For many years I have waited for a man who could overcome the power of my magic. Long years ago, a prophet told me that such a man would one day come and that his name would be Odysseus."

"I am that man, Circe, and if it pleases you, I would like to remain on your island for some time. My men are weary of the sea and are in need of rest."

"Ah, your men," said Circe, "Not one minute more shall I wait. Come with me, Odysseus, and I shall restore your men to their proper form."

She did as she had promised, and the men could hardly praise Odysseus enough for saving them. At first they were too frightened to come near Circe, but after a while they came to love and admire her as much as Odysseus. The rest of the crew soon came out from their hiding places in the wood, and that very night everyone celebrated with a feast. Circe had at her command the nymphs of river and wood, and she proved a most delightful hostess.

Indeed, so delightful did she prove to be that before anyone knew it, eleven months had come and gone. Circe's table never ran short of food nor her cellar of wine. The men laughed and feasted, and their thoughts of Ithaca faded away like mist over the water. Even Alex and Stacey nearly forgot their home and the job they had been given by Pan. Day in and day out they swam in the ocean and stretched out on the warm white sand. Circe's island was truly a paradise.

But when a year had passed, Alex and Stacey remembered once more why they had been sent to accompany Odysseus, and they asked to have a meeting with him later that night.

"Odysseus," said Alex, when evening had come and they were alone, "it is time that we sailed off for Ithaca. If we do not leave now, we never will."

"Yes," said Stacey, "you must remember Penelope and Telemachus. I'm sure that they long for you every night. We cannot stay here any longer."

"But life is so pleasant here, and I am sick of the sea."

"Odysseus!" said Alex more strongly, "did we escape from the cave of the Cyclops and the land of the Laestrygonians only to rot away here on an island far from Ithaca? That was not your thought when you left Troy. You have a family to care for and a kingdom to run. You can't stay here and forget about all your responsibilities. What would happen to society and to civilization if we all threw off our duties? It's time to go home."

"Surely you children have been sent by the goddess Athena. I am ashamed now that I stayed here so long. Go call my crew and tell them to prepare the ship. Tomorrow we sail for Ithaca. But now let me go and break the news to Circe. I know that her heart will be sore."

While the children went to rouse up the men, Odysseus went in search of Circe. When he had told her what was on his mind, she was very sad and wept for many minutes. But she soon dried her tears; in her heart, she knew that Odysseus would have to leave soon.

"But, Odysseus," she said, "before you go, there is a thing I must tell you. I had hoped I would never have to share this news with you, but now it seems that I must. You must not attempt to sail to Ithaca until first you have visited the land of the dead. There, in that dark place of shadows, you must meet with the spirit of Tiresias (tie REE see us), the blind prophet of Thebes. He will speak to you words of warning that you must hear and obey if you are to make it safely back to your own land."

When Odysseus told his men that they would be sailing tomorrow not for Ithaca but for Hades, they all groaned and their hearts nearly failed them. But they were strong sailors, all of them, and by morning they had resolved themselves to follow their captain wherever he led them.

♦ ♦ ♦

The island of the Laestrygonians rises from the sea in a land of almost perpetual day; the rocky shore along which lies the entrance to Hades is hidden away in a land of eternal night. To this grim and mournful shore, Odysseus guided his ship with a map that Circe had given him. When they had landed and pulled their ship on the sand, Odysseus ordered his men to stay in the boat and went on ahead accompanied only by Alex and Stacey. Making use once again of Stacey's pearl, the three of them entered the dark cave whose steps led down to the final abode of the dead. For some reason unknown to the children, Odysseus had also brought with them a lamb and a goat. They would soon discover why.

As they reached the bottom of the stairs, the ghostly shades of a dozen men and women glided over to them. When he saw the shades, Odysseus drew out his knife and slit the throats of the lamb and the goat. He drained their blood into a large cauldron that lay at the bottom of the stairs. The smell of the fresh blood rose up in the air, and the shades immediately flocked to the cauldron as though they would drink from it. But Odysseus, who had been told beforehand by Circe what to do, stood between the cauldron and the shades and held them back with his sword.

"None may drink," he said, "but Tiresias."

Slowly a tall slender shade who carried what looked like a cane was led forward by the shade of a boy. The elder man bent over the cauldron and drank deeply of the blood. As he did, his ghostly body seemed to grow firmer and to become almost solid, and he began to speak:

"Odysseus, I thank you for allowing me to drink of the blood. Here in Hades we flit around like ghosts, and many of us cannot even remember our own names. But when we drink the blood, our memories return, and the weight of flesh is restored to our empty bodies."

"O great Tiresias, Circe the enchantress has sent me here to ask of you what dangers lie ahead for me as I make my way back to Ithaca."

"There are three further dangers that await you, Odysseus. First you must sail your ship past the isle of the Sirens. As you do, the Sirens will sing out to you in voices so sweet and lovely that you will be driven mad by it and will steer your ship toward their isle that you might listen to them forever. But do not do so. If you do, your ship will be dashed on the rocks, and there you and your men will lie lifeless, victims of the Sirens' song.

"Next, you must navigate your ship through a narrow strait of water. On either side of the straight, a fierce creature lies in wait. The first, Scylla (SKILL ah), has six heads and lives hidden high in a cave. If you pass too near her shore, her heads will fly out, and in each of her mouths, she will snatch one of your sailors. The second, Charybdis (ka RIB diss), is a sea serpent who lives deep down in an underwater cavern. Many times throughout the day, she sucks the water above her into her giant throat and spits it out again. When she does, a whirlpool of tremendous force is formed that destroys anything that comes near it. If you take my advice, you will hug the shore of Scylla. Better to lose six men than to risk your entire crew.

"Finally, if you can avoid it, make no landing on the island of the sun. But if you must, be sure you do not touch the cattle that live there, for they are sacred to the sun. If in your folly you devour any of the cattle, it is certain that none of your crew will return to Ithaca alive.

"But now, Odysseus, I have a word to speak into your ear. If you make it home alive, you will not find Ithaca as you left it. By the time you return, evil men will have wormed their way into your home. They will call themselves suitors for the hand of your wife, Penelope, but most of them will spend their days eating your food and abusing your servants. They will even try to talk your son, Telemachus, into joining them in their gluttony. But you must pray that he does not give in to their pleas. If he does so, or if Penelope agrees to marry one of them before your return, all will be lost for you. Be on your guard. The world is not now as it was when you sailed for Troy so many years ago."

"What do you mean, Tiresias? How has it changed?"

"Then you have not heard. Betrayal and treachery are everywhere. No longer can one tell the true from the false. Justice and virtue have gone from the hearts of many. The Lord Agamemnon discovered this himself when he returned home in victory, only to be killed that very night by his wife and her lover. It is up to you, Odysseus, and to your loyal wife and noble son, to restore faith and honor to a world that has forgotten both."

"It's the Accuser again," Alex whispered to Stacey.

"Ah, my boy," said Tiresias, "I can see that you too are a prophet. But it is best not to speak his name. Rather, you must help Odysseus to return to Ithaca and set his house back in order. By doing so, he will pass on to those who come after him a vision of the good life that shall help to keep many generations on track. For there is nothing finer or nobler than when a man and a women who share one heart and mind live together as husband and wife, and their generosity and love spread out to all those who come to their home. On the foundation of such domestic bliss shall many great nations be built.

"But now it is time that you three must leave this place of shadows and return to the world of the living. Even now, I feel the shades pressing at my back, eager to drink the blood from the cauldron. If you do not flee at once, I fear they will overwhelm you."

As he spoke, the shades moved as one toward the cauldron, and the faces of Odysseus and the children grew green with fear. Stacey lifted high her necklace, and the glow from the pearl blinded the eyes of the shades. By the time they could see again, Alex, Stacey, and Odysseus were back on board, and the ship was sailing full speed toward the lands of sunshine and warmth.

21

Dangers at Sea

For three days the mist of Hades seemed to cling to the sides of the ship, but on the fourth, the sun returned in all its glory, and the crew sang praises to Zeus that they had survived their trip to the land of the dead. Odysseus, afraid that his men might mutiny if they knew the dangers that lay ahead, did not share with them the warnings of Tiresias. Best, he thought, if he dealt with these problems on his own.

When the seventh dawn had stretched out her rosy fingers across the sky, the ship found herself riding the rocky coast that led by the island of the Sirens. The children had hoped that Odysseus would find some alternate route by which he could avoid the Sirens and their deadly song, but it soon became clear that there was no other passage they could take.

"Children," said Odysseus, "I fear these Sirens shall capture my crew with their song and that we all shall be dashed against the rocks."

"Well," said Stacey, "one time Daddy took us to his University for a big carnival that they held out on the grass. When it started to get dark, a band set up their instruments and started to play."

"Oh, I remember, Stacey; they were *so loud* I thought my ears would fall off."

"That's right, Alex. Don't you remember what we did? We stuck our fingers in our ears and blocked out the sound."

"Of course, Stacey, that's a great idea. Odysseus, why don't you just have your men stick their fingers in their ears?"

"That's a fine idea, though I'm afraid it won't block out the sound fully enough. But if I melt down some candles and place the warm wax in their ears, then they won't be able to hear anything, not even if we shout at them."

"And what about us, Odysseus," said Stacey, "we'll have to have wax in our ears too."

"Nonsense!" said Odysseus, "I mean to hear this Siren song."

"But if you do," continued Stacey, "the song will drive you mad, and you will force your men to row the ship toward the Sirens."

"Very well," said Odysseus, "then I shall instruct my men to tie me tightly to the mast and to ignore whatever signals I give them. If I motion to them to sail toward the shore, then they must tie me all the tighter and row as fast as they can. Yes, this I shall do, and if you two children would also like to hear the Siren song, than I shall have you both bound to the prow of the ship."

"Hooray!" said Stacey, "I can't wait to hear their song. I'll bet it's prettier than any of my music boxes."

Odysseus proceeded to put his plan into effect, and before they knew it, the children were tied tightly to the mast, and the ship was gliding smoothly along the coast. Up ahead, the isle of the Sirens glowed red and green in the evening sun. The Sirens themselves had lovely faces, and their eyes and lips were painted in rich colors; but their bodies were like those of birds, and their toes and their fingers were as long and sharp as the talons of vultures. Just as the smell of a freshly-baked apple pie rises up from the windowsill and tickles the noses of those who pass by, so the song of the Sirens floated gently on the air and wrapped itself about the ears of Odysseus and the children:

Ah mariner weary and sore,
    Who sailest by star and by sun,
In search of that sweet, golden shore
    Where the traveler's journey is done.

Come hither, pay heed to our song,
    To pause and to listen is best;
The ocean is cruel and long,
    But here there is comfort and rest.

To toil is for oxen and mules,
    What are you, a man or a beast?
Leave striving to rich men and fools,
    'Tis sweeter to sleep and to feast.

Our tales are as old as the sand,
    We know all that has passed on the sea:
Listen! you *shall* understand;
    Listen! and set your heart free.

The song was more beautiful than anything the children had ever heard. It made them want to laugh and cry all at once. It made them want to forget everything and everyone they knew and to spend the rest of their lives listening to the song over and over again. If it weren't for the ropes that bound them, they would have thrown themselves into the sea and swum a hundred miles just to hear it one last time as the water closed over their heads.

Odysseus too was entranced by the song, and he signaled madly to his men to turn the ship toward the isle. But they only tied him more tightly to the mast and beat at the foam with their oars. As the ship glided swiftly over the water, the sailors looked toward the isle from which they had escaped and saw the broken timbers and torn sails of countless ships. Rocks jutted up all along the shore, and upon each of them hung a human skull washed clean by the tide. Not until the island was less than a speck in the distance did the crew cease their rowing. The song faded away on the breeze, and the three listeners slowly regained their sanity. Still, many times over the next few days, a phrase from the song would flow into their heads, and it was all they could do to stop themselves from jumping overboard and swimming back to the misty, body-strewn isle of the Sirens.

The next few days of sailing were uneventful ones, and the crew spent much of their time relaxing on the deck and trading memories of Ithaca. For awhile, Odysseus hoped against hope that the twin monsters Tiresias had warned him about might only be myths to frighten sailors. But alas, the prophet had spoken truthfully. From atop the crow's-nest, a sailor cried out to Odysseus the words he had long dreaded to hear:

"Narrow strait ahead, captain."

Though Odysseus knew it was impossible to sail past Scylla and Charybdis without falling victim to one of the monsters, he was not a man to give up easily. He ordered his men to hug closely the coast of Scylla and then positioned himself carefully on the side of the ship nearest the coast. With spear in hand, he focused his eye on the entrance to the cave where dwelt the six-headed monster. At the first sign of movement, he swore he would hurl his spear into the neck of Scylla. It was a good plan, and it might even have worked, had not Charybdis chosen that very moment to suck in the waters around him. The sucking caused a great roaring to rise up from the sea, and Odysseus, startled by the sound, turned his head to look. A second later he re-fixed his eye upon the cave, but it was too late. With the speed of a hawk, the ever-hungry Scylla had shot out her six heads and grabbed hold of six members of Odysseus' crew. As swiftly as they had shot out, the heads recoiled backwards into the cave. The six hapless men felt themselves being pulled upwards, and, as they soared to their grisly deaths, they stretched out their hands and called out the name of Odysseus.

For days after the incident, Odysseus remained locked in his cabin and would talk to no one. The horror of those six faces crying out to him in their fear and agony was almost more than he could bear. But the sea has a way of pushing memories into the past, and the smell of the fresh salt water slowly revived the grief-stricken captain.

"Men," he said, after many days had passed, "I knew of the danger of Scylla and Charybdis but kept it from you lest you lost your courage and refused to sail on. But now I shall speak plainly to you of one final danger. Though I hope to avoid landing on the island of the sun, if land there we must, there is something of which you need to be warned. On the island is a herd of cattle sacred to the sun god. As long as you do not touch them, we will be safe, but if, in your folly you eat of their flesh, swift destruction will fall upon you."

The men all swore they would never do such a thing, and Odysseus breathed a sigh of relief. But when the next day brought a calm sea and no breeze, and the days that followed brought the same, he began to worry. When a week had passed and still there was neither wind nor current, Odysseus knew that the ship would now have to land at the first port of call. Fate, it seemed, would not allow him to pass by the island of the sun without at least a brief landing.

Reminding his men once more of their promise, Odysseus disembarked and set up camp along the shore. With the help of the crew, he soon found a stream with fresh water and filled up the buckets on the ship. The men then searched the island for food, but none was to be found. Odysseus, sensing danger, was about to order his men to get back on board, when a storm rose over the sea, and they were forced to run for cover. The rain soon stopped, but the winds continued to blow so strongly that it was impossible to sail away from the island. For seven days, the winds blew, and the ship rocked wildly in the bay. On the eight, the men, whose supplies of food had long run out, began to starve. Odysseus, hoping to find a deer or boar on the other side of the island, took his bow and left for a day of hunting.

The moment he was gone, the men began to grumble amongst themselves:

"What do I care for Odysseus' warnings? Anything, even drowning at sea, is better than starving to death on an island rich with cattle."

"If we only eat one, perhaps the sun god won't notice."

"It's worth the risk. If we don't eat soon, we will die anyway."

Alex and Stacey tried to reason with them, but the men refused to listen. Instead, they seized the children and locked them up in the hold of the ship. Then, with Odysseus gone and the children out of the way, the men fell upon the cattle. They cut up the meat into strips and then wrapped the strips around long branches which they slowly rotated over an open fire. The men ate quickly without speaking to one another, hoping that the sun, which had been hidden for some time behind a bank of clouds, would not notice what they had done.

But the sun, whose eye sees all that passes on this wicked world, saw their deed and grew red with anger. As the men continued to feast, the meat fell off their sticks and began to crawl on the ground as if it were alive. The sound of cattle lowing in the field rose up from the fire, and the men's faces grew green with fear. Hoping to find some means of escape, they lifted their eyes and saw the figure of Odysseus advancing toward them with the carcass of a deer slung over his shoulders.

"What have you done!" he cried, "What folly has driven you to this madness! Here I have brought you fresh meat to fill your bellies, and I find you feasting on what should not be eaten. And listen men! Even now I hear the winds dying away. Perhaps if we depart quickly on the next tide, you can outrun your doom, though I doubt that such a thing is possible now."

Like men who flee from a ghost that they can neither hear nor see, Odysseus and his crew hoisted high the sails and drove their ship as fast as it could go across the wine-dark sea. But wherever they turned in their mad flight, the sun pursued them from its lofty chariot in the sky. One moment the skies were clear; the next, storm clouds billowed on the horizon.

And the rains descended, and the floods rose, and the winds blew, and beat upon the ship. And great was its fall and its destruction. As chaff is scattered to the wind by the thresher's flail, so Odysseus' men, one by one, were tossed from the ship and sank like lead into the sea.

As for Odysseus and the children, the sun took pity on them. As they struggled to hold themselves above the waves, the mast of the ship, naked now of all its ropes and sails, floated by them. Eagerly, the three of them grabbed on to it and were carried swiftly away from the wrecked ship and the storm that had wrecked it. For three days they floated on the mast, but on the fourth, they looked ahead and saw the narrow strait of Scylla and Charybdis. The current drove them to the side of Charybdis, and as they passed over the underground cavern of the beast, they heard the great sea monster roar. In a matter of seconds, he would begin to suck in the water, and all of them would be pulled down to a watery death.

"We are all doomed," cried Odysseus, and lifted his right arm toward the sky.

What happened next took not only Odysseus but Alex by surprise. Without saying a word, Stacey pulled the pearl from off her necklace and swallowed it whole. Then, taking a deep breath, she cast herself into the sea and began swimming downward toward the cavern of Charybdis. Her small lungs quickly ran out of oxygen, but Stacey was not afraid. Trusting in the words of Thetis and the power of the pearl, she opened her mouth and breathed in the water. Normally, such an action would have killed her instantly, but by now the pearl had taken effect. In and out of her mouth the water rushed, and Stacey found to her delight that she was now breathing like a fish. Indeed, with each "breath" of water, she felt herself growing stronger, and her eyes, which a moment before had seen only darkness, saw clearly and distinctly to the very bottom of the strait.

But there was something else, something that Thetis had forgotten to mention. As Stacey kicked her legs behind her, she felt a strange twitch run along both her thighs and pass down like lightning through her knees. The force of the twitch drove her feet together, and for a second Stacey was almost knocked off balance. The water swirled wildly about her legs and drove them closer and closer together until there was not an inch of space between them. What happened next is rather hard to describe. Both her legs turned outwards so that the heels of her two feet touched and her toes stretched out in opposite directions. Her thighs and knees flattened out, and green scales started to form under her waist. Like a troop of dancing fairies, the scales ran up and down her legs, crisscrossing and interweaving in a thousand delicate patterns.

A bolt of pure energy shot through Stacey's body, and she kicked as hard as she could. This time, however, the kick began not in her thighs but in her waist, and in response not two skinny legs but a wide, firm fin beat hard against the water. The motion propelled her forward as swiftly and as smoothly as a dolphin. Twice more she kicked her fin and found herself poised before the cavern of Charybdis. Unafraid, she swam headfirst into the cave, only to be met by the purple-green, snake-like head of a giant sea serpent in the very process of sucking water into its long, dark mouth. Stacey threw back her head and twisted her waist; the movement caused her fin to whip around sharply and sent it smashing into the face of the beast.

Charybdis was stunned by the blow, and his mouth went slack. Stacey, seeing that she had succeeded in stopping the monster from drowning her friends, swam out of the cave and shot upward toward the mast. But the serpent was too quick for her. His enormous tail snaked its slimy way out of the cavern and wrapped itself around Stacey's chest. With a terrible sinking feeling, Stacey felt herself being pulled back to the bottom of the sea. She struggled as hard as she could, but the thick, coiling body of Charybdis was holding her too tightly.

Down, down she sank, until she was but a mere ten feet away from the waiting jaws of the beast. In utter desperation, she opened her mouth wide, bent down her neck, and bit the serpent. At first nothing happened, for the pain of the bite took several seconds to reach the brain of the beast. But when the signal finally arrived, the body of the serpent shuddered, and its grip around Stacey loosened by a fraction of an inch. The memory of her three years of ballet class flooded back into her mind, and Stacey stretched out her body and began to spin furiously.

After what seemed like five minutes, but was only five seconds, her body moved upward about six inches. At that rate, Stacey thought, she would never break free. But she was wrong. The very moment the coils of the serpent slipped past her waist and came in contact with her scales, Stacey shot upward like a ball out of a cannon. Scales, it seemed, were much more slippery than she had thought. In no time at all, her face popped out of the water, and she swam over to the mast.

"Move apart, boys!" she yelled, and Alex and Odysseus, excited and shocked at once to hear Stacey's voice, did as she asked. Stacey held her hands in front of her and took a firm grip on the center of the mast. Then, with all the energy she could muster, she began to kick her fin up and down, up and down. She, the boys, and the mast, went skidding over the water as fast as a ship under full sail. Alex glanced over his shoulder at the top of Stacey's fin flipping in the water and cried out in disbelief:

"Stacey, you're a mermaid!"

"I know," she said with a big smile, and then put her head under the water and kicked even harder. Behind them, they heard the roar of the waters being sucked into the mouth of Charybdis, but by then, Stacey had pushed them so far away that the whirlpool was powerless to reach them.

"Way to go, Stacey!" said Alex, "You've saved us all!"

For the next twenty minutes, Stacey continued to act the part of an outdoor motor, and the mast, along with its passengers, was carried miles and miles across the sea. But when the last speck of the pearl had dissolved in her throat, and the magic had all flown away, Stacey felt a shudder run down the center of her fin. She pulled her head out of the water, took a deep breath of air, and kicked her fin one last time. But this time when she kicked, it was not the tail of a mermaid but the two legs of a girl that splashed against the water. Exhausted and exhilarated all at once, Stacey pulled herself up onto the mast and let her feet dangle gently over the side.

"Stacey," said Odysseus, "your courage is like that of Athena herself. If ever I return to Ithaca, I shall instruct my minstrel to recite a song of your exploits beneath the sea."

"That's OK," said Stacey, "I've always wanted to be a mermaid, even if it was only for thirty minutes. I'm just sad that my pearl is gone; now I have nothing to remember Thetis by."

"Yes you do, Stacey," said Alex, removing the corral ring from his finger, "The liquid is all gone, but the ring is still beautiful. You can keep it for as long as you want."

"Thank you, Alex. I'm gonna put it on now and never take it off again."

The children would have said more to each other, but they were interrupted by the voice of Odysseus, who was shouting out on the top of his lungs:

"Land ho!"

Stepping Out of the Shadow

Odysseus and the children washed ashore on the small but lovely island of the nymph Calypso. She greeted the strangers with a warm welcome and fed them until their bellies could hold no more. After dinner, Calypso sat by the side of Odysseus and stared into his eyes like a schoolgirl in love. She begged him to recount his adventures, and he, being a good guest, told her all that had befallen him since his departure from Troy.

Having already lived through the adventures, and sensing that Calypso wanted to be alone with Odysseus, Alex and Stacey quietly left the house and took a long, lazy stroll along the beach. The evening was so still they could hear the crabs scuttling back and forth on the sand and the breeze whistling through the leaves of the palm trees. But when they had reached the opposite side of the island, and the house of Calypso could no longer be seen, the silence of the night was ripped apart by a great whirring in the air. The children froze and looked up into the sky. A large object was hurtling toward them at an amazing speed.

It was the deck.

As the children watched with eyes wide open, Pan landed the deck gently on the soft sand and jumped out onto the beach.

"Another job well done, children. You have brought Odysseus safely to the island of Calypso and have helped him to survive the two threats that might have prevented him."

"*Two* threats?" said Alex with a puzzled look on his face.

"Of course, Alex. As you yourself once told Odysseus, the danger of accepting a false homecoming is as great a threat to the man seeking to return home as are the many dangers to his body. Circe and the lotus-eaters were perhaps greater obstacles than the Cyclops and Scylla. But I repeat, the dangers have been met and overcome. Here on this island Odysseus will remain hidden for the next seven years, and Calypso will do everything she can to convince him to forget Ithaca and take her as his wife. She will even promise to make him immortal. But in the end, Odysseus will remember what you helped him to learn. When the time is ripe, he will leave this island and, after another brief stay on another false Ithaca and another meeting with another false Penelope, he will finally make his way to his own dear country.

"Unfortunately, by the time he arrives, things will be in a state of turmoil. As you heard Polyphemus threaten in his curse, and as you heard Tiresias warn in his prophecy, the palace will have been overrun by evil guests in the form of an ill-bred, riotous group of suitors for the hand of the fair Penelope. And it is to that strife-ridden palace that we must now make our way.

"Telemachus, who was only an infant when Odysseus left for Troy, has almost reached his twentieth year, and his heart has all but given up hope of ever seeing his father. The evil ways of the suitors with their endless eating and drinking have worn away at his noble spirit, and he begins to doubt himself. You have helped the father; now you must help the son. You must do all in your power to convince him that he, like his father, can be a hero: that he can rise above the evil and treachery of his age and live the life of virtue and honor.

"But come, it is time to board the deck. The fan has started to spin, and the wooden boards have begun to vibrate. We must travel seven years into the future and across the depths of the sea to the rugged island of Ithaca."

Alex and Stacey leaped aboard, and the deck went soaring into the night air.

♦ ♦ ♦

Being the son of a hero is no easy task, especially if your father has been gone for nineteen years, and you have no memories of him at all. People who meet you on the street or in the town square and are told that you are the child of a celebrity immediately begin to judge you and to measure you against the tales of your famous father. "Will you be as great as he was?" their searching eyes seem to ask, "Will you prove as brave and as strong?" The best way to handle such pressure is to seek out other children of famous parents and form a group. Better yet, you might meet with the equally heroic friends of your heroic father and ask them to help guide you in the noble ways of your family.

Alas, Telemachus had neither. He had never met a single companion of the great Odysseus, and there were no young men on the island of Ithaca who could help to encourage him on the road to virtue. To the contrary, every afternoon and again every night, the palace of his father was overrun by a band of suitors with the table manners of a herd of pigs.

Luckily, at least, there was his mother, Penelope. She was horrified by the very thought of marrying one of the suitors and spent most of her day shut up in her room. She was a woman of great faith and patience and had a streak of cleverness that rivaled that of Odysseus himself. She had, for example, come up with a number of tricks to hold the suitors at bay until the long-awaited return of her husband. Telemachus' favorite trick was the one about the burial shroud.

One day, Penelope had come before the suitors with a grave look on her face and told them that as an obedient daughter-in-law, it was her duty to weave on her loom a large and costly shroud with which to bury her father-in-law when the day of his death arrived. Only after she had done so would she consider marrying again. Thinking this a task that would take no time at all, the suitors agreed and stopped pressuring her to marry one of them. Each day, in the sight of the suitors, Penelope worked hard at her loom, but each night, while the palace slept, she undid what she had woven the day before. For three years, she continued this trick (which just goes to show you how truly stupid the suitors were), but in the end, she was betrayed by one of her own maids. Her trick exposed, the suitors pressed her all the harder until Penelope could not bear to come down into the dining hall of the palace.

Meanwhile, as the days and weeks dragged on and Odysseus did not return, the suitors became more and more bold. Treating Odysseus' house as if it were their own, they raided his wine cellar and stripped his kitchen of all its food. When the fancy took them, they would order the farmers who worked Odysseus' land to bring them the finest pigs and sheep. Without paying back Penelope for her livestock or even thanking her, they would then slaughter the animals in plain view of all and feast on their flesh.

This was the state of affairs in the palace of Odysseus when Telemachus looked up from his supper to see two young strangers enter the hall. The children looked hungry and tired, and the moment they entered they walked over to the suitors and asked them if they could have something to eat. The suitors merely laughed at the children and, even though the food wasn't theirs to begin with, refused to give them even a crumb. When Telemachus saw this, he was shocked and stricken at heart and ran immediately over to the children:

"Dear strangers, beloved of Zeus to whom all guests are sacred, forgive me for the rude behavior of those wicked men. None of them belong to this family or to this house. Rather they are hangers-on who steal our food and treat our servants with disrespect."

"If that is so," said Alex, "why don't you chase them from your house and bar the doors behind them?"

"Alas, if only my father, Odysseus, were here, he would drive these wicked men away. But who am I to do such a thing? I am no hero or soldier like that great man they say is my father, though for me I sometimes doubt if I am really his son."

"Telemachus," said Alex in a strong voice, "it is your own father, along with the goddess Athena, who has sent us here to rouse you to action. You are no longer a child. It is time you threw off the influence of these suitors and made a thorough search for your father. If you find that he is still alive, you must prepare things for his return. But if you learn that he has died, you yourself must rid your house of these suitors."

When Alex had finished speaking, Telemachus cast his eyes upward and exclaimed:

"Praise be to Zeus. Now I know that Athena is with me even as she was with my father before me."

No sooner did the words escape his lips than the sky thundered and a bolt of lightning struck the courtyard outside the hall. At the sound of the thunder, the faces of the suitors grew pale, but Telemachus' eyes flashed, and he felt within his chest the strength of a hundred men. Like a man new born, he strode into the dining hall and addressed the suitors:

"How can any man bear to be in the same room with such as you? You feast on food that is not yours and drink the wine for which you have not worked. But do not deceive yourselves; soon you shall get your just rewards. I go now through Ithaca to see if there are any young men left on this island who respect the codes and the virtues of our fathers. However many I find, I shall take them with me on a ship and sail on the morning tide in search of my father. Pray that you are not still in this house on the day that I return with him."

The suitors were taken aback, and many shook so nervously that they spilled their own wine on their laps. But one of the suitors, whose name was Antinous (an TIN ouss), found his tongue and approached Telemachus:

"Ah, my fiery young hero, what strong words you speak to us. But let us put aside old grudges and grievances. Come, sit and drink with us, and we shall do just as you say."

"Antinous, do not think that you can drag me down to your level. I would be ashamed to sit in the company of such men who steal the property of another man and insult his wife."

When they heard Telemachus' words, all the suitors growled and gnashed their teeth, but they did nothing to try to stop him. Like all bullies, they were really cowards at heart. Their grumbling, however, did not go unnoticed. As Telemachus slowly made his way to the passage that led out onto the courtyard, he heard the sound of a door closing on the landing above.

It was Penelope. She had heard the commotion and was coming down to see what was happening. The long years of waiting for Odysseus had done nothing to spoil her beauty, which was as fresh and alluring as it had been on the day of her wedding. Like Andromache and Hecuba, her eyes had the look of one who watches, but in the face of Penelope, this eternal stare carried with it a wilder, almost playful spirit. One minute she was there, her feet planted firmly on the earth; the next minute, you might almost imagine her floating away. When she looked down from the top of the staircase and saw Telemachus heading out the door, she cried out:

"Son, where are you going? What is happening down there?"

"Mother," said Telemachus with firmness, "it is not right that you should come down here while these shameless men are in the hall. Return to your chamber and take up your work at the loom. But you must leave me free to do the work of a man and protect this house from scoundrels and villains like these."

Penelope was taken aback. Never before had Telemachus spoken to her so forcefully. She grabbed a hold of the railing, and a look of sadness spread over her face. And yet, at the very same time, there ran through her eyes a flash of joy and even triumph. Her son had finally become a man. Without saying another word, she returned to her room and took up the shuttle in her hand.

For the next six hours, Telemachus, with Alex and Stacey by his side, searched through the streets of Ithaca for men to accompany him on his journey. To his surprise and delight, he soon discovered that all young men were not like the suitors. Many there still were who yearned to do noble and heroic deeds and to follow the path of virtue.

As rosy-fingered dawn spread through the sky, Telemachus, the children, and a new crew of eager sailors pushed off into the sea. Their destination was the palace of King Menelaus and Queen Helen. Surely thought Telemachus, if anyone might have news of his father, it would be Menelaus. For the first time in his life, he was going to meet a real live hero!

◆ ◆ ◆

The sea journey was a long one, and Telemachus spent much of it conversing with the children. Despite his new found courage, he still suffered from much anxiety and healthy doses of insecurity and self-doubt. Though he longed to meet Menelaus face-to-face, he was also terribly nervous that he would do or say something to embarrass himself in front of the legendary warrior. He had never had anyone to teach him the proper way for sons of heroes to behave. How could he possibly stand up to the test?

"Telemachus," said Stacey after they had been at sea for many days, "I know a little bit how you feel. I'm the youngest in the family, and my brother has always done very well in school. Sometimes

I'm nervous when I meet one of Alex's old teachers. I'm afraid she will measure me against Alex and expect me to be just like him. But Daddy told me once that each of us is different and that we each have our own gifts and talents."

"But the pressure is so great. Sometimes I'm afraid it will crush me."

"Do you have something I can write on the deck with?"

"Certainly," said Telemachus and handed her a soft white stone, "but what is it you wish to draw for me?"

"Last year, Daddy took Alex and me outside and gave us each a piece of chalk. He told us that we were about to draw on the ground a picture of what a true hero is like. First, he had us make a huge circle and then draw directly in the center of it a stick figure. Daddy said what he was about to show us was true for boy heroes and girl heroes alike, so he let me add long hair and eyelashes to my stick figure! Next, he had us draw four arrows outside the circle so that their points all pressed down on the sides of the circle. Finally, he had us draw another four arrows inside the circle with their points pressing outward as if they would pierce right through it.

"'There,' he said, 'you have two pictures of a hero and a heroine. The arrows pressing down are all the forces and pressures that he must bear up under: fate, duty, the reputation of his parents, the attacks of his enemies, the will of heaven, and so forth. The arrows pushing outward are his own inner strength and courage that he uses to assert who he is and what he was made for. Those arrows are his virtues and his talents, his honor and his nobility, his yearnings, his visions and his dreams.'

"When Daddy paused for a moment, Alex jumped in and asked why the man didn't just step out of the circle and prevent himself from having to bear up under all that weight. But Daddy answered that if he were to do such a thing, he would cease to be human. Yes, he would be free, but he would no longer be the man or woman he had been created to be.

"Finally, Daddy told us that there was a verse—I think it was from the Bible—that summed up everything that the picture represented. I remember that part because as he said the verse out loud, he grabbed hold of a stick and pointed it back and forth from the outer arrows to the inner arrows. Let's see if I can remember it: 'We are troubled on every side, yet not distressed; we are perplexed, but... but...'"

"'... but not in despair,'" added Alex, "'Persecuted, but not forsaken; cast down, but not destroyed.' I remember it too, Stacey. I think the man who said that verse was named Paul. You wouldn't know about him, Telemachus, but like you, he once took a great sea journey and even survived a shipwreck. I don't remember all the details, but I do remember that when Paul had finished all of his journeys and his adventures, he was able to write to a friend that he had fought a good fight, that he had run a straight course, and that he had kept the faith."

"Oh that I could say such a thing when my labors are finished! Oh that my father might be here to say it with me!"

"Never fear, Telemachus," said Alex, "we have met your father in person, and we have both noticed already how much you are like him in form and voice. I'm quite sure that Menelaus and Helen will feel the same way when they meet you."

And, indeed, Alex's prophecy came true. Even before he could tell the King and Queen of Sparta his name, Helen commented to her husband how strongly he resembled Odysseus. His manner of walking, the curve of his brow, and even the way he moved his hands when he spoke were exactly like those of his father.

For three nights in a row, Telemachus feasted on the finest food and wine, and Menelaus shared with him countless tales of the Trojan War. Telemachus listened intently to all that he said, but he rejoiced most fully when he heard of the great wisdom that Odysseus showed in all his years at Troy.

"Good King Menelaus," Telemachus said, "in your palace I have not only learned of the courage and resourcefulness of my father, but I have learned something else as well. For years now my mother has urged me to fight off the suitors who are making a mockery of my home, and now these children have urged me to do the same. But I found it difficult to find the strength to perform such a deed, for I had no sense of what I would be fighting *for*. Never in my life have I seen a palace as peaceful and noble as your own. Never before have I witnessed the proper relationship between a guest and his host. Now that I see what a home can and should be, I feel all the more eager to drive out these suitors and establish such a home."

"As a matter of fact, Telemachus," said Menelaus, "I *have* heard that things are not well at your palace and that a group of suitors have overrun your home."

"Ah me," thought Telemachus, "is my shame known even in this far country?" But out loud to Menelaus, he merely replied: "Yes the rumors you have heard are true. In fact, it is for this very reason that I have come to visit your court. Neither I nor my mother has had any word of Odysseus. You, however, were his companion at Troy, and so I hoped that you would know something of his whereabouts."

"Alas, my boy," replied Menelaus, "I have only recently returned to Sparta myself. For eight years, I and my crew have been driven through the lands of Egypt and Ethiopia and even to the shores of Libya. But I did, during my travels, receive brief word of your father.

While stranded in Egypt, I learned that Proteus (PRO tee us), the Old Man of the Sea, dwelt nearby and would speak of future things to any man who could catch him. Securing the help of his daughter, I leaped upon Proteus while he was sunning himself, like a seal, upon the beach. The moment I grabbed him, Proteus—to whom is given the power to change his shape at will—transformed himself into a large bear. My first reaction was to release him and run for my life, but Proteus' daughter had warned me that her father would try such a ruse and that if I could continue to hold on to him through all his various transformations, I would conquer him. This I did, but it was no easy task. Again and again he changed his shape, from a bird to a mouse to a great and golden lion. He even turned himself into a block of ice and a pillar of fire. But still I held. In the end, Proteus returned to his original form and I released him.

"From him I learned the wonderful news that I myself would not go to Hades after death but would be taken to the Elysian (ee LIZ ee an) Fields, where it is always spring and the heroes of old walk back and forth on the green grass sharing stories and speaking together of glory and virtue. I was told too of the fate of the other Greek warriors, including the sad news of my own brother, Agamemnon, who had no sooner returned home when he was murdered by his own wife and her lover. As for Odysseus, I was told that he was being held on the island of Calypso, a lovely nymph who longed to keep him there as her husband. Still, though Proteus did not reveal all, it was clear to me that Odysseus would not remain much longer on the island but would return soon to Ithaca.

"But now, Telemachus, though I greatly desire to keep you here with us in Sparta, I must advise you to return home without delay. It is not good that Penelope be left alone for too long. She is a noble wife and a faithful one, and yet think of how Agamemnon's wife was led astray and forgot her marriage vows. I feel confident that Odysseus shall not remain much longer from his home, but if he does not return, then it is up to you, Telemachus, to rid your house of these suitors. Have you not heard of Orestes (oh RES tees), the son of Agamemnon? Once he had grown to manhood, he returned to the palace of his murdered father and killed the man who had led his mother astray. Now you, Telemachus—and what a splendid young man you have grown to be—must find within yourself the courage and wisdom of Orestes. Then future ages shall sing your glory, and you shall be known as a greater man even than your father."

"That," said Telemachus, "is my greatest desire. Oh that I might be like Orestes and show myself worthy to follow in the footsteps of my father."

"That you shall be, my boy, I have no doubt. But before you go, a last word of advice. Remember the story of Proteus. The world is no longer the place it was before we sailed to Troy. All now is deceit, treachery, and disguise. Be ye not fooled by appearances! Hold on tight to what you know is true, no matter how many phony disguises are thrown up before you. If you can endure and learn to see through the mask, you shall save yourself and your household as well."

With that, Menelaus and Helen, being the noble hosts that they were, loaded Telemachus' ship with costly gifts of gold and hand-worked ivory. If time had permitted, Telemachus would have gladly stayed with them for another year, but his duty and his destiny constrained him. It was time for him to return home.

— Chapter —

23

The Faithful and
the Unfaithful

Spending so many months at sea with Odysseus had trained Alex
and Stacey to scan the horizon and to pick out even the smallest
of details. It was a discipline that they now used to great purpose.
Whereas all the other sailors saw only the blue sky and the blue sea,
the children spotted far in the distance, just behind a rocky reef, the
prow of a ship. It was clear that the ship was attempting to hide itself
from view, but the trained eyes of the children were not so easily
fooled. They immediately told Telemachus what they had seen, and

the son of Odysseus, whose cleverness seemed to grow by the minute, concluded that the hidden ship could belong to only one crew: the suitors. The cowards and scoundrels that they were, the suitors had hired a ship and were now lying in wait to ambush Telemachus as he returned home. The suitors had seen the change in Telemachus and were eager to get rid of him before he became a threat.

But here was one fish that would not fall into their net. Pulling out his sea chart and checking the position of the sun, Telemachus turned his ship off course and took a different route back to Ithaca. The moment he landed, his first thought was to run back to the palace and check on Penelope, but the children dissuaded him from such a reckless course of action.

"If the suitors have already set one ambush," said Alex, "they may set another. It is better that you should hide yourself for a while from the palace. Are there any of your father's older servants whom you still trust? Has anyone remained loyal to their old master?"

"Of course," said Telemachus, "I should have thought of that myself. There is only one place I can go now: the hut of Eumaeus (you MAY us)."

"Eumaeus?" asked Stacey.

"Yes," said Telemachus with a smile, "he is my father's swineherd and has been since before I was born. All these years he has been like a second father to me. He protects his pigs as a good shepherd does his sheep, and the suitors have given up trying to take pigs away from *him* to eat at their feasts. He is truly a prince among swineherds. How fondly I remember all those long evenings by the fire listening to Eumaeus' stories. He is quite a good storyteller, and I think he knows more tall tales than anyone else alive. He told me once that the nights on Ithaca were long ones and that one could either spend them sleeping or sharing memories over food and wine with one's dear companions. It was he who convinced me that too much sleep was a bad thing and that even memories of grief and pain grow all the sweeter when remembered together.

"But you should know that he also has a tendency to be very suspicious. As you can imagine, every few months for the last eight years, some traveler or merchant or beggar has found his way to the palace and tried to win over Penelope with stories about her husband. They knew such stories would secure them rich gifts from my mother, and indeed, they always did. But Eumaeus hated these impostors and always did whatever he could to expose them for the lying cheats that they were. As for me, well, I let them tell their tales; my mother was always happier and more content after hearing their made-up accounts of Odysseus. I never saw the harm in it."

"Telemachus," said Alex, "you can trust us. We are not like those impostors. We really have seen your father, and we can assure you that he will be home soon."

"I believe you, children," said Telemachus, "Convincing Eumaeus, though, will be a different matter. There is his cottage now beneath that great oak tree. You two stand by the door while I knock and see if he is home."

But Telemachus never got a chance to knock. Before he got within ten feet of the cottage, the door swung open, and Eumaeus came running out:

"Young master," he cried, taking Telemachus in his arms and crushing him in a bear hug, "you have returned home safely! I was told of the suitor's plot to ambush you but could find no way to warn you. Truly the goddess Athena has shown you favor as she did to your father before you."

"She has indeed, good Eumaeus," said Telemachus and stepped aside to reveal Alex and Stacey. "She sent me these two children to help me in my journey, and it was they who spotted the ship hiding behind the rocks."

"What fine-looking children," said Eumaeus, "but you both must be starving. My cottage is a humble one, but anything I have is yours. Please come in where we will be safe and no one can overhear what we say."

All four of them slipped quietly into the cottage and sat down at Eumaeus' table. To their surprise, they quickly discovered that they were not alone. In a corner of the cottage, there sat an old beggar wearing a tattered robe and carrying a gnarled walking stick. His hair was white and stringy, and his body was covered with sores and bruises. Though weak now and frail, the children could tell by the muscles bulging out from under his robe that he must have been a man of strength in his younger days. His face was creased with wrinkles and his beard scraggly and unkempt, yet there was a strange fire in his eyes that seemed almost familiar to the children.

"Telemachus," said Eumaeus, "I would like you to meet my guest. He is a stranger on Ithaca and has already been abused badly by the suitors. Though I offered him bread to eat and wine to drink, he preferred not to abuse my hospitality and spent his day yesterday begging from the suitors. All he got for his pains was curses and a few rotten vegetables. One of them, may the dog rot in Hades, even hurled his stool at the head of the stranger. He has just now returned to the cottage, and we have been discussing things that you will find of interest. This stranger comes with news of your father. Any day now, he will arrive back in Ithaca."

"But Eumaeus," said Telemachus, "are you saying that you believe him? This is certainly a turn of events. Does he bring proof that can convince even you?"

"He does, my prince, he does. But don't take my word for it. Speak to him yourself."

"Good stranger," said Telemachus, turning his gaze in the direction of the beggar, "is it true that you have news of my father? Can it really be that he shall return soon?"

"Nothing now can stop him from returning," said the beggar, "But tell me, young man, why do you permit such evil suitors to turn your house upside down? Why have you not yet driven them out?"

"Such things are easier said than done, stranger. What can I, a single man, do against so many? I will wait instead for my father to return. He will know what to do."

"Then you are not yet ready," said the beggar, and walked toward the door as if he would leave the cottage.

"No, Telemachus," yelled Stacey, "don't let him go. Remember the advice of Menelaus. There is something not right about that beggar. Grab a hold of him and do not let him go."

With a great lunge, Telemachus leapt across the room and threw his arms around the stranger. "No," he said, "I shall not let you go until you tell me all that you know. I am ready now to begin plotting against these suitors whether or not my father is here. I am the Prince of Ithaca and will someday be her king. Reveal to me at once all that is in your mind."

"Ah," said the beggar, turning to face Telemachus and staring him directly in the eyes, "*now* you are truly my son."

"What did you ..."

But before Telemachus could finish his sentence, a swirl of light dropped from the ceiling and wrapped itself around the beggar as if it were a cloak of fire. Immediately, a change came over him. His white hair turned dark brown, and the wrinkles in his face and bruises on his skin all smoothed themselves out and disappeared.

His tattered robe was transformed into a white toga, and his whole body grew straighter and taller than it had been a moment ago.

"Odysseus!" cried Alex, "Hooray! I thought there was something familiar about your eyes. Here we were in the same room with you all of this time and did not even know it."

"It is well you did not," said Odysseus, "My disguise was made by the goddess Athena herself. Even Eumaeus did not know me until I revealed myself and asked him to help me test you, Telemachus. Ah what a noble man you have grown into. Together, there is nothing that can stop us. From this moment, the days of the suitors are numbered."

But that was all he had time to say. After staring at Odysseus in frozen wonder and asking himself if this were not all a dream, Telemachus had thrown off all of his doubts and fears and had begun hugging and kissing his father. It was a glorious reunion, one that made all the dangers that Alex and Stacey had faced since the day they had been carried to Troy seem richly repaid.

Like two sailors who have been separated for nineteen years by rough seas and the designs of fate and who are then reunited in the twentieth, Odysseus and Telemachus sat close by each other and traded stories of their struggles and triumphs. But when they had finished and the passion for it had left their hearts and minds, Odysseus rose and addressed his son:

"Now, Telemachus, is the time for action. You must go at once to Penelope and remind her of a pledge that I had her make before I left for Troy. The pledge was this: that if I had not returned by the time you had become a man and thrown aside all childish ways, she would chose a husband from the noble families of Troy and marry again. Though she will no doubt be loath to marry one of the suitors, tell her that she can at least ensure a strong mate if she gathers together the suitors in the hall and has them take part in a contest for her hand. But by no means are you to tell her that you have seen and spoken to me. If she is still the faithful and clever wife I left twenty years ago, she will do this thing though it makes her heart sore. Then, when all has been set in motion, return to me here and we shall go together to the palace."

Before Odysseus could finish speaking, Telemachus was already out the door. This was a day the young hero would not soon forget.

♦ ♦ ♦

Many years before the birth of his son, Odysseus had entertained in his palace a noble man from a neighboring island. Together they had hunted and feasted and traded tales, and before the man returned to his home, guest and host had exchanged gifts. To the man, Odysseus had given a sword and shield of the finest craftsmanship, while to Odysseus was given the gift of a magnificent bow. Odysseus never took this bow into war, but left it always hanging on the mantle in his great hall. It had been made of the finest wood and was so large and stiff that Odysseus alone had the strength to bend and string it. Many times over the last twenty years Penelope had stared lovingly at it, longing to see Odysseus string it once again. No better or more appropriate test, she now thought, could there be than to have the suitors try their strength on the bow of Odysseus.

True to the promise she had made to her husband, Penelope sent word to all the suitors that that very evening they were to assemble in the great hall for a contest. She herself would be the prize, and the winner would become her new husband. Then, because her craft was as great as that of Odysseus, she added to her announcement that the suitors, one and all, were to bring with them the kinds of rich presents that suitors normally bring to those they wish to marry. By such a ruse, she hoped to plunder the suitors and restore to her palace the wealth that they themselves had stolen away. Telemachus, who shared in the cleverness and foresight of his parents, added his own provision to the announcement:

"Gentlemen," he said with a concealed smile, "tonight at the contest I fear that you will all get drunk and wild, and if this happens, it is very possible that you may injure each other with your swords. Therefore, I propose that you all lay aside your weapons before you enter the hall, and I will instruct my servants to hold them safely in a closet until morning."

The suitors, foolish as ever, were won over by Telemachus' words and agreed to strip themselves of all weapons before entering the palace. This done, Telemachus raced back to the cottage of Eumaeus and told his father of all the preparations that had been made. By this time, Athena had transformed Odysseus back into the guise of the old beggar so that he might more easily slip unnoticed into the hall. Bidding farewell to Eumaeus and thanking him again for his loyalty and courage, father and son, along with brother and sister, set out for the palace.

As they passed through the courtyard on their way to the great hall, Odysseus spotted the small, sickly figure of a dog. It lay on a pile of dung, left behind by the donkeys and mules that had been tied there while their riders conducted their business indoors. Odysseus recognized the dog at once (his name was Argus), and a large tear formed in his eye. When Argus heard the sound of Odysseus' voice speaking to Telemachus and looked upon his old master with half-closed eyes, he immediately lifted up his head and barked twice.

"My faithful dog," thought Odysseus in his heart, "only you were not fooled by my disguise. How often did you and I share in the hunt in those peaceful days before Troy!"

With a gentle smile on his wrinkled face, Odysseus bent over to pet the dog, but he was already dead. The long wait for his master was over. Argus had expired in peace. Wiping the tears from his eyes lest his true identity be exposed, Odysseus strode into the hall, Telemachus and the children at his side.

If the courtyard was peaceful and quiet, the inside of the palace was all a flurry with activity. The bow had been brought down from its place on the mantle and was mounted on a large table in the center of the hall. Nearby, a set of axes had been driven into the ground in intervals of five feet. The handles of the axes each had a hole in them about the size of a silver dollar. The rules of the contest as laid down by Penelope were that the winner must not only string the bow, but shoot an arrow through the holes in the axes. To win Penelope as his bride, the victor would have to show himself both strong and skillful.

Most of the suitors had already arrived and had laid their expensive gifts before Penelope. They ignored Telemachus and his guests and walked around flexing their muscles and bragging as to how they would win the contest. When the last of the suitors had appeared, Penelope took the gifts to her chamber and left the proceedings in the hands of her son. Then the great doors of the hall were shut, and the contest began.

The first to take a try at the bow was none other than Telemachus himself. By so doing, he hoped to intimidate the suitors. Three times he pressed down on the bow and almost strung it, but before he could attach the string, the bow snapped out of his hand. But on the fourth, he pressed with all his strength and would surely have strung the bow had not his father signaled to him to stop.

"Ah well," said Telemachus, "I guess my strength is not equal to that of Odysseus." The suitors all gave a sigh of relief when he had said this, but Alex, Stacey, and above all Odysseus had seen and known that Telemachus was indeed the equal of his father.

One by one, starting with Antinous, the suitors took the bow in their hands and attempted to string it. They grunted and groaned and made every possible excuse, but not one of them came even close to stringing it. Desperate to succeed, some of the suitors rubbed the bow with oil, others with soap, and even others with milk. But to no avail.

When all the suitors had been given a try, Odysseus, still disguised as an old beggar, stood up and asked to be given a chance at the bow. The suitors were furious and threatened to throw him out, but Telemachus put up his hand and said that the stranger would be given a chance. As Odysseus stepped forward and lifted the bow, Alex and Stacey both held their breath. They thought that Odysseus would string it at once, but instead he turned the bow around and around in his hands checking to see if any worms or ants had burrowed into the wood. Next, he took grease in his hand and rubbed it on the bow until it shone like glass. Finally, as easily and as quickly as a guitarist puts a string on his instrument, Odysseus strung the bow and gave it a firm pluck. Immediately, a sound like the song of a bird rang out throughout the hall; it was like the note a swallow sings as he returns to the place of his birth in search of his mate. A bronze-tipped arrow lay on the table beside where the bow had been. Odysseus took it up in his hand and notched it to the string. Crouching down near the floor, he lined up his bow with the first of the axe handles and shot. The arrow soared through the first of the holes and continued straight on through all the axe handles.

When they saw that the old beggar had not only strung the bow but shot it with expert precision, the suitors all turned pale, and some ran to the door in hopes of slipping out quietly. But such an escape was not to be granted them. While the contest had been going on in the hall, Telemachus' few remaining loyal servants had bolted the doors on the outside. The Day of Judgment had come, and none would be spared. With a great leap, Odysseus sprang onto the table and removed from under his cloak a quiver full of arrows. As he did so, his disguise fell away, and all recognized that this was no elderly beggar but a king in his prime.

"So," he said in a voice that shook the walls, "you thought in your folly and pride that I would never return. You thought that you could steal my wife and trample my property under your feet. Now, wicked suitors, you shall receive the just reward that is your due."

With that, Odysseus drew an arrow from the quiver, notched it on the string, and sent it flying toward Antinous. The arrow caught him just as he was lifting a glass of wine to his lips and passed clean through his neck. Antinous fell to the floor, and the red wine poured over him like blood. With their leader gone, the suitors scattered in panic and tried to hide in the corners of the hall. But nothing could protect them from the arrows of Odysseus. As the pitiless suitors cried out for pity, Telemachus drew from its hiding place another bow and joined Odysseus on the table. Together, father and son emptied their quivers into the hearts and bellies and necks of the suitors.

As the massacre continued, one of the wicked servants who had feasted many a time with the suitors and who had treated his own fellow servants with contempt, tried to slip out a secret passage and lay hands on the suitors' weapons. Alex and Stacey saw him and followed him to the closet where the weapons were being kept. The servant hoped to smuggle the weapons down to the suitors so that they could surround Odysseus and Telemachus and kill them. Even now he was walking softly down the stairs to the hall, his arms filled with swords, spears, and bows. Unfortunately for him, he hadn't reckoned on the cleverness of the children. As he reached the midway point of the stairs, Alex and Stacey each took a spear in hand and hurled it at him. They were not aiming for his head, but his feet. As they had hoped, the spears struck him hard on the ankles and caused him to miss the next step. Like a large rock that comes loose from the top of a mountain and rolls down the hill, causing an avalanche to form behind it, the wicked servant tumbled down the stairs followed closely by a multitude of bronze and wooden weapons. There was, however, one particularly sharp sword that beat him to the bottom of the stairs. Upon that sword his body fell, and the point was driven through his chest.

Seeing that the servant was dead and the danger that he posed was now gone, Alex and Stacey rushed back into the hall. Still the suitors ran in terror; still the hero and his son drew their arrows and shot. It seemed to Alex that not even a man with a machine gun could kill as fast and as accurately as Odysseus and Telemachus were doing with their bows.

When the last of the suitors had fallen, and the sound of screaming men had died away, Stacey saw upon the face of Telemachus a look that frightened her. It seemed for a moment as if the son of Odysseus would begin to exult in the bloodshed and defile the bodies of the dead suitors. In the eyes of Odysseus, Alex saw an equal savagery that seemed eager to extend the slaughter to the fathers and brothers of the suitors he had killed. A heavy presence began to fill the room, bringing with it the smell of death and of destruction.

"No!" cried Stacey and ran to the side of Telemachus, "you must let your anger go. If you do not, the Accuser will take root in your mind and never release you."

"And you, Odysseus," cried Alex, "must take the sword out of your heart. The guilty have paid for their crimes. Remember Achilles and do not press beyond the mark of justice. You have rescued your house. Now make an end to the bloodshed."

Little by little, the anger and fury drained out of the tired, sweaty faces of Odysseus and Telemachus. And as it did, the presence the children had felt lifted and was gone.

"Come," said Odysseus, "we must return the bodies of the dead to their families. No more shall suffer or die for the sins of these wicked men. And instruct the serving maids that they are to take sulfur and lime and scrub clean this floor until not a trace of blood is left. So shall my house be purged and peace and order restored to the land of Ithaca."

The Marriage Bed

While the battle raged in the hall below, Penelope had been sitting quietly in her chamber weaving a bright tapestry on her loom. In and out the shuttle flew binding together the silken threads as one does a bundle of sticks. Suddenly, from the other side of the door, a sound of great rejoicing rose up the stairs. Penelope carefully hooked the shuttle to the loom and rushed out to the top of the landing.

"Milady," said a voice from below, "your husband has returned and has killed the suitors. Telemachus too was with him in the hall, and together they accomplished the deed."

Penelope shook her head and reached out for the banister. Was she awake or dreaming? Could the news be true or was it merely a cruel trick concocted by the suitors who had lost the contest? Still, even if it were a trick, she would have to investigate. Slowly, like one who walks in a trance, she glided down the staircase. At the bottom stood her son with two children at his side. And there was another: a man whose eyes seemed to stare ever forward like her own.

"It is I, Penelope," said the man, "I have come home."

Odysseus thought that Penelope would rush immediately into his arms, but instead she paused and stared at him closely.

"You look very much like the man I remember," she said, "but how can I be sure. For so long now I have guarded myself against men who would trick me into breaking my bridal vows. No, I shall not allow my heart to hope until I am sure. Tonight, stranger, you shall stay here in the palace, and tomorrow I shall question you more closely to make sure you are my own dear husband for whose return I have long awaited."

Penelope then turned to her right and signaled to her maid to come to her. When she had come, Penelope spoke to her in a loud voice so that all could hear:

"Take two butlers with you and go at once to the master bedroom. You must take a hold of the bed and drag it out into the hallway so that this stranger can sleep on it until morning."

No sooner had the words left her mouth, than the face of Odysseus turned red with rage, and he cried out:

"What! Who has dared to move our bed? Certainly no man or even a group of men could have performed such a feat. A great secret went into the making of that bed, a secret known only to Penelope and myself. That bed I made with my own two hands to celebrate the day of our wedding. An olive tree once grew beneath this room with a trunk three times thicker than the largest wagon wheel. Around that trunk I built this room and crowned it with a ceiling inlaid with gold and silver. I next removed the branches from the tree and trimmed the trunk until it rose a full two feet above the floor. With my axe and my saw I shaped the trunk into a bed, and there it has remained these many long years. Tell me quickly, good lady, if that bed has truly been moved. If so, it can only be the work of a god."

When Odysseus had finished, the face of Penelope grew flushed, and her knees began to tremble. Great tears streamed down her cheeks, and she threw herself into the arms of her husband. "Odysseus," she said through her tears, "do not be angry with me that I have tested you in this way. You yourself have taught me to use my wits and to survive by cunning."

"Dearest wife," said Odysseus, "the time for cunning is now past. Goodness and truth shall now reign in this palace and throughout my entire kingdom. Where the wives of Menelaus and of Agamemnon failed their lords and allowed passion to cloud their thinking, you alone have remained steadfast and true. Many generations shall sing your praises, and you shall be the mother of all faithful wives who come after you. But come now, my beloved, our bridal chamber awaits. I have much to tell you, and I long to lie again by your side."

With one graceful sweep of his arms, Odysseus lifted Penelope from the floor and carried her off. The children stood for awhile in the hall and spoke softly with Telemachus until their eyes could barely stay open and their lips could barely move. When he saw how tired they were, the son of Odysseus, fine host that he was, led them to a great chamber with walls of marble and twin beds carved out of ivory and studded with jade and mother of pearl.

For ten long and peaceful hours, Alex and Stacey slept soundly, but when they awoke and looked out the window, the moon was still high in the sky. Though they knew it not, the goddess Athena, out of her great love for Odysseus and Penelope, had held back the dawn an extra twelve hours so that husband and wife might have all the time they needed to share their stories and express their love. And to ensure that they not be disturbed, she had instructed the god of sleep to throw his cloak about the palace and hold everyone but the loving couple in the sweet arms of slumber.

When it comes to children, however, the god of sleep has limited powers at best, and Alex and Stacey thus woke to find themselves alone in a deserted palace. Drawn by a strange impulse, they walked together out into the silent courtyard. There, by the side of the fountain, was the deck, its fan beating against the air like four wide oars that dip in and out of the wine-dark sea.

"Quick," said Pan, "we must not delay. Even as Athena holds back the dawn, so have I been holding back the night in your own kingdom of Houston. If we are swift, we should be able to arrive before sunrise."

◆ ◆ ◆

Though on most summer mornings, Mommy got up first and then went upstairs to wake the children, this morning it was Mommy and Daddy who were catapulted out of their slumber by the shock of two little bodies bouncing on to their bed.

"We're back," cried Alex and Stacey together, "we're back. Jinx, personal jinx!"

"What is all that racket?" said Daddy, who did *not* like to get up early, "Have my two children just lost their minds?"

"No, Daddy," said Alex, "we're not crazy. We're heroes. We just got back from saving Western civilization."

"He's right, Daddy," said Stacey, "thanks to us, all the "bounda-tions" are back in place."

"That's *foun*dations, Stacey," said Alex, and then burst into a fit of laughter.

"That's what I said, Alex!" screamed Stacey, and immediately began kicking his legs and his stomach with her feet.

"Alright, alright," said Daddy, "You obviously have some great adventure to tell us about, and there's only one place for telling adventures."

"The cave!" shouted Stacey, "The cave!"

"Exactly," said Daddy, and then lifted up high the bed sheets so that all four of them could crawl underneath. When Mommy, Daddy, and the two children were all huddled together at the foot of the bed, Daddy draped the sheets over their heads and everything went dark.

"I'm scared, Alex," said Stacey, "I feel like I'm in the Cyclops' cave again."

"The Cyclops' cave?" said Daddy, "What have you two been up to?"

"Well, Daddy," said Alex, "it's a long story." And then, taking turns so that each got to tell his favorite part, Alex and Stacey recounted all that had happened to them since they first heard Pan bumping around in Stacey's closet. And, strange as it may seem, at the very same time they were telling their adventures to their parents, far away in Ithaca Odysseus was telling his own adventures to his wife.

When they were done, Daddy was speechless—which didn't happen very often—and gave his two little heroes a tight squeeze.

But by the time evening had rolled around, and Alex and Stacey were getting ready for bed, Daddy had found his voice again.

"Children," he asked, "did I ever tell you what first made me want to be a storyteller?"

"No, Daddy," said Stacey, "you never did."

"Well, believe it or not, it was the *Odyssey*. When Homer introduced me to Eumaeus, and that prince among swineherds said that it was far better to stay up all night and tell stories than it was to sleep, I knew that I was hooked. I've been staying up late telling stories ever since."

"But we really met Eumaeus, Daddy," said Alex.

"I know," said Daddy, "And that's why I'm convinced that you two kids will grow up to be even greater storytellers than your father."

"Daddy," said Stacey, "now I can't wait for you to tell us all the stories from the *Iliad* and *Odyssey*. Will Alex and I be in the stories?"

"No, sweetie, you won't. When Homer tells it, most of the things that you and your brother did will be attributed to Athena or Zeus or one of the other gods who dwell on Mount Olympus. And many of the things you taught to Achilles and Odysseus will be left out all together. Homer's world just wasn't ready for some of those things."

"Yes, Daddy," said Alex, "that's just what I told Achilles. But what about Pan, Daddy? Will he remember what I taught him about faith, hope, and love?"

"Yes, Alex," said Daddy, "I think that he will remember some of it. But when the long-awaited one finally comes, then Pan will disappear into the forest, and all the prophets and oracles of Greece will cease. Until that time, however, Pan will hold up what you taught him as a tiny light in the darkness."

"Like a candle you mean?" said Alex,

"Exactly, Alex," said Daddy with a look of pride on his face, "Exactly!"

It was now quite late, and so Daddy shut off the light, tucked the kids in their beds, and prayed, as he always did, that they would have a good night sleep without any nightmares and that no monsters or goblins or ghosts would bother them while they slept.

And this time, God answered his prayer.

The Gates of Freedom

For the third time that afternoon, Alex and Stacey looked at each other, burst into a double grin, and began to sing, at the top of their lungs, "The Ballad of Davy Crockett." For you see, Alex had just graduated from fifth grade, and, to celebrate, his family had decided to spend the weekend in a city Alex had always wanted to visit. They had left Houston that morning at 11:30 (Daddy wasn't much of a morning person!), and they were now less than an hour away from their longed-for destination: San Antonio.

San Antonio!

The very name was magical, like one of those secret passwords that opens hidden doors on the sides of ancient hills. Speak it once, and the hills begin to shake; speak it twice, and the rocks are ripped apart, revealing within wonders untold: buried treasure, mysteries forgotten, adventures perilous.

◆ ◆ ◆

The Alamo was even more wonderful than Alex and Stacey had imagined. Though much of the long, circular wall that had once surrounded the mission was gone, there was still enough of it left to give the children a sense of what the battle must have been like. Even better, the fact that so much of it had crumbled away and that only portions of it were left made it seem much, much older than it actually was. In reality, the battle of the Alamo was fought less than 200 years ago and the mission itself had been built less than 200 years before that, but as Alex and Stacey gazed on the remains of the Alamo, it seemed to them like one of the many ruins they had seen three years earlier when they had visited Greece with their mother. That, of course, was during that magical summer when the two children had been drawn back, by the power of the dreaming stone and a set of panpipes, into the world of Greek mythology.

What a summer that had been! While their school friends were swimming at the community pool and riding their bikes, Alex and Stacey were helping Perseus to kill the dreaded Medusa, accompanying Orpheus to the Underworld, and fighting the Minotaur with that most noble of heroes, Theseus. And if that were not adventure enough for a lifetime, when the next summer rolled around, Alex and Stacey were taken back once again to ancient Greece where they met the mighty heroes of the Trojan War and the beautiful women who loved and suffered for them. Though Alex was only nine at the time and Stacey only eight, they had both shown great courage and faith: in the face of a hidden, but deadly evil, they had not only taught Achilles to put away his wrath but had helped to reunite the loyal family of Odysseus. And by so doing, they had, wonder of wonders, helped to save civilization itself!

Well, as you might imagine, when the next summer arrived, Alex and Stacey were half expecting that they would be drawn back again into the misty world of Greek mythology. Indeed, every time they peered over the top of a hill or opened a rusty door or strained their eyes to see the end of a rainbow, they were sure, *quite* sure, that

Pan or Theseus or maybe even Zeus himself would appear out of nowhere and invite them back into the land of legends. The world was full of magic, their Daddy had taught them: they just needed eyes to see it and ears to hear it—and a nose to smell it, Stacey would often add. But, alas, there was nothing to be seen that summer. The magic, it seemed, had all gone away. Had they grown too old, they wondered? Perhaps their help was no longer needed?

◆ ◆ ◆

Alex and Stacey were supposed to be listening to the tour guide as he spoke passionately to a group of tourists about the last tragic days of the Alamo. But since the two children already knew all the details—Daddy was a better storyteller than any old tour guide—they quickly grew restless. To be honest, there was only one thing that they really wanted to do, only one thing that any true, red-blooded kid wants to do: explore! And I must say that the Alamo is a great place for exploring. Stony paths run off in every direction, leading you now to open, grassy spaces, now to secluded spots hidden along the corners of the wall. Only a few feet away, on the other side of the wall, the modern noises of San Antonio rushed by, but that only made it all the more strange. It was like discovering your own secret garden right in the middle of a bustling city. As for Alex and Stacey, their favorite parts were the long covered walkways and the maze of connected rooms that had been built right into the wall.

"Alex," said Stacey, when they had broken away from the group and were strolling along one of the walkways, "Do you think Davy Crockett stood on the same path we're on now?"

"I'm sure of it, Stacey," said Alex, "His spirit is all over this place. Didn't you feel it when we first walked through the chapel?

And when we saw all those flags representing the states that Davy and the others came from? I wouldn't be surprised if this whole place were haunted."

"Alex," said Stacey, in a whisper so low he could barely hear her, "Do you think we could go back … back to the battle … just like we went back to Troy?"

"Oh, Stacey, let's not think about that again. There are no dreaming stones here, and I can't imagine Pan will be popping out of the wall anytime soon. Let's just forget about it."

"No!" insisted Stacey, "I won't forget about it! It was me who found the dreaming stone three years ago, and it will be me who will find something else today." And with that Stacey ran off toward one of the doors that led into the maze of rooms.

"Oh, brother," said Alex, "here she goes again." He had half a mind to leave her behind and return to the tour group and to his parents, but he still loved that crazy sister of his and worried about her quite a bit. So he did the only thing he could do: he ran off after her.

Ten minutes later, having chased his sister through every room of the Alamo, Alex finally found her sitting on the grass with her head cradled in her hands. He could tell she was upset, and so he didn't tease her or even ask her what she was crying about. Instead, he took her hand gently and told her that if it would help, he would do some searching too. "C'mon" he said, "We'll look together—you take that side of the wall and I'll take this side. Make sure you search every inch of it; you never know what might be hiding between the stones."

Stacey stopped crying immediately and began running her hands up and down the wall. Alex did the same, and for several minutes neither child said a word. They barely breathed. You see, they were concentrating very hard. Then, at the same exact moment, they both shouted: "Hey, what's this?"

One minute they had each been staring at a blank wall. The next minute there they were—two coonskin hats hanging like stockings from two rusty nails driven into the wall. As quickly as you can say, "remember the Alamo," Alex and Stacey swept the hats off of the nails and placed them firmly on their heads. Then Alex ran over to Stacey and gave her such a big hug that it lifted her right off of the ground.

"I can't believe it, Stacey," he shouted, "You were right. Maybe there is some magic left after all. But what do we do now?"

"I think we should spin, Alex. Remember two years ago when we found Pan hiding in my bedroom closet? He told us that he had traveled back in time by spinning so fast and hard that his tail grew and wrapped itself around him. I'll bet if we hold hands and spin together like we used to do when we played "ring around the rosy" that something magical would happen."

"No way, Stacey," said Alex, "You know that I hate spinning rides."

"No, Alex, it will be OK. You just have to believe."

Alex didn't like the idea at all, but Stacey insisted so hard that he finally gave in. Taking her right hand in his left and her left hand in his right, he began shuffling his feet to the right.

"Faster, Alex," said Stacey, "Faster!" With a sigh, Alex began to move his feet quicker and quicker. Stacey too picked up her pace and soon the two of them were whipping around like one of those spinning gates that you find in old playgrounds.

"Whee!" shouted Stacey, "This is more fun than ballet class."

And still they spun faster. And as they did, the two tails on their coonskin hats lifted higher and higher until they were pointing straight out behind their heads. As if they were living things, the tails began to hum loudly in the breeze, making a sound like a thousand crickets on a warm summer evening. And as they hummed, they began to glow: a deep green glow that radiated out from the ends of the tails and circled itself around the spinning children.

Soon, Alex and Stacey were moving so fast that if anyone had tried looking at them, he would have seen only a blur. Think of the four blades of a ceiling fan. When the fan is moving slowly, you can see each of the blades distinctly, but when the fan shifts into high speed, it soon becomes impossible to distinguish one blade from the other. In the same way, as the children's speed increased, it became more and more difficult to tell where Alex left off and Stacey began.

And still they spun faster, until all you could see was the green glow growing brighter and brighter. Locked inside that whirling green tornado, Alex and Stacey closed their eyes as tightly as they could and prayed that they wouldn't faint. The humming from the tails had grown so loud that it blocked out every other sound; it was like being locked up in the engine of a jet.

Then, just when the humming become so loud that Alex and Stacey were sure they would go deaf, a loud explosion cut through the air. Immediately, the humming stopped, the green glow disappeared, and Alex and Stacey were flung down to the ground.

"What was that explosion, Alex?" asked Stacey, after her head had stopped spinning.

"I'm not sure, Stacey," said Alex, as he blinked his eyes several times and rubbed the back of his neck, "It sort of sounded like fireworks."

Instantly, the explosion sounded again, and the children were left with no doubts as to what had caused it. It was a cannon!

Sensing the danger, the two children leaped to their feet and began looking wildly around them. They were in the middle of a battle. Men with rifles in their hands and knives in their belts were running in every direction. Everywhere there was shouting and screaming, and everywhere the noise of cannons and gunfire echoed in the still air. Alex and Stacey could tell by the sky that it was very early in the morning. The men around them looked tired and disheveled, as if they had all been aroused suddenly out of a very deep sleep.

Alex and Stacey were afraid they would be run over in all the madness, but nobody came near them or even seemed to notice them. Slowly, cautiously, they began to walk toward the wall. As they did, they studied more closely their surroundings. To their amazement, they discovered that the walls of the Alamo had grown; they now stretched around them in a huge circle. All along the wall, as far as the eye could see, they saw a series of low roofs and men lying on the roofs with their rifles propped up on the edge of the wall. When you looked at the faces of those men, you could tell they were afraid, and yet there was also a calm about them. They seemed to know in their hearts that they were in the right place at the right time, that this, somehow, was their destiny.

And then they saw *him*! There he was, less than ten feet away, with his coonskin hat on his head and his rifle clutched tightly in his hand. He was leaping from roof to roof, shouting orders to his men, and firing his rifle at the oncoming soldiers. As they got closer to the wall, Alex and Stacey could see that the invading soldiers were carrying makeshift ladders over their heads. Dodging bullets and stones, each would lean his ladder up against the wall; when the ladders were secure, two or three other soldiers would scramble up each of them as fast as they could.

Their plan, of course, was to leap over the wall and get inside the courtyard of the Alamo. But Davy Crockett wasn't about to let *that* happen. Each time the head of a Mexican soldier appeared above the wall, Davy would hit him with the butt of his rifle, sending him and the ladder flying back to the ground. He was a whirlwind of energy. At one point, Alex and Stacey watched in awe as Davy—in the space of only five seconds—shot one climbing soldier with his rifle, then turned it around and hit a second with the butt, and then kicked a third with the bottom of his right foot. One, two, three, the soldiers and their ladders crashed into the dirt. It was an amazing sight, so amazing that the children almost forgot to breathe.

After thirty minutes of heavy fighting, there was a brief lull in the battle, and Davy sat down to catch his breath. Immediately, Alex ran over to him and put out his right hand.

"Mr. Crockett," he said, "that was the finest shooting I've ever seen."

But Davy didn't shake his hand or even answer him back. In fact, he looked right through Alex as if he weren't there.

"That's not fair!" shouted Alex, clenching his fists with anger and frustration, "We come all the way back in time to the battle of the Alamo, and I can't even talk to Davy Crockett. Why should we be brought back here, if we can't talk with anyone?"

"Why don't we try shouting together, Alex?" said Stacey.

Alex nodded his head in agreement, and the two children began yelling out Davy's name on the top of their lungs. Anyone who had heard them would have had a headache for the next hour, but the yelling made no impression at all on Davy Crockett.

"Save your strength, children," said a voice behind them, "Davy cannot hear you. None of them can hear or see you. You are but two invisible onlookers here."

The sound of the voice startled Alex and Stacey, and they immediately swung around. Behind them stood the largest and strongest man they had ever seen. His legs were like massive tree trunks whose roots run deep into the earth; upon them rose a belly and chest that, to the children at least, appeared wider and thicker than the walls of the Alamo. His right hand was extended in greeting, while his left, as solid and powerful as the mast of a ship, clutched tightly a gnarled club. At first, the children thought that he was wearing a coonskin hat like Davy and a dark cloak, but when they looked more closely, they realized that the furry thing on his head was the face and mane of a lion and that what they thought was a cape was, in fact, the lion's shaggy hide. Though he was the one hero that Alex and Stacey had not met on their two journeys to ancient Greece, Alex knew at once who he was.

He was Hercules.

✦ ✦ ✦

About the Author

Louis Markos holds a BA in English and History from Colgate University and an MA and PhD in English from the University of Michigan. He is a Professor of English and Scholar in Residence at Houston Baptist University, where he teaches courses on British Romantic and Victorian Poetry and Prose, the Classics, C. S. Lewis and J. R. R. Tolkien, and Art and Film. Dr. Markos holds the Robert H. Ray Chair in Humanities and lectures on Ancient Greece and Rome, the Early Church and Middle Ages, the Renaissance and Romanticism for HBU's Honors College.

He is the author of sixteen books: *A Worldview Guide to the* Iliad, *A Worldview Guide to the* Odyssey, *A Worldview Guide to the* Aeneid, *From A to Z to Middle-Earth with J. R. R. Tolkien, The Dreaming Stone, From A to Z to Narnia with C. S. Lewis, C. S. Lewis: An Apologist for Education, Heaven & Hell: Visions of the Afterlife in the Western Poetic Tradition, On the Shoulders of Hobbits: The Road to Virtue with Tolkien and Lewis, Literature: A Student's Guide, Apologetics for the Twenty First Century, Restoring Beauty: The Good, the True, and the Beautiful in the Writings of C. S. Lewis, The Eye of the Beholder: How to See the World like a Romantic Poet, From Achilles to Christ: Why Christians Should Read the Pagan Classics, Pressing Forward: Alfred, Lord Tennyson and the Victorian Age,* and *Lewis*

Agonistes: How C. S. Lewis can Train us to Wrestle with the Modern and Postmodern World. All these books are available at his amazon. com author page: https://www.amazon.com/author/louismarkos

In addition to books, he has produced two lecture series with The Teaching Company, *The Life and Writings of C. S. Lewis; From Plato to Postmodernism: Understanding the Essence of Literature and the Role of the Author* (available at www.teach12.com). He has published over 150 book chapters, essays, and reviews in various magazines and journals, given well over 300 public lectures in some two dozen states as well as Rome, Oxford, and British Columbia, and had his adaptations of The *Iphigenia in Tauris* of Euripides, The *Helen* of Euripides, and The *Electra* of Sophocles performed off-Broadway. He is committed to the concept of the Professor as Public Educator and believes that knowledge must not be walled up in the Academy but must be disseminated to all who have ears to hear. Visit his webpage at: www.Loumarkos.com

About the Illustrator

A native of Sugar Land, Texas, Angela Merkle has long been fascinated with illustrating fantastic worlds and characters. She started drawing as soon as she could hold a pencil and has not stopped since that age. As a young adult she attended Houston Baptist University, where she earned a Bachelor of Arts in Art and Writing. After receiving her degree, she worked in the sign industry for six years, first as a customer service representative, and then as a graphic designer.

Angela has been commissioned for many art and graphic design projects, including wedding invitations, acrylic paintings, book cover illustration, pencil portraits, logo creation, t-shirt designs, property illustration, original character design, various print items, and much more. She now works full time at Houston Baptist University as an administrative assistant, continuing her artistic work in her free time.

Angela currently resides in Sugar Land near her parents. She has an older brother who lives in Katy, Texas, and an older sister who lives in Baton Rouge, Louisiana.

More examples of her work can be seen on her website, www.angelamerkleart.com

THE
DREAMING
STONE

ALSO AVAILABLE
by Louis Markos

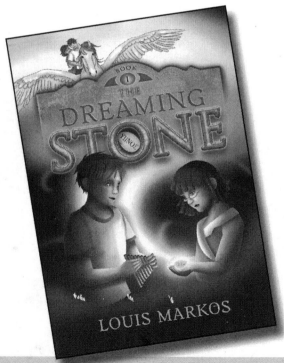

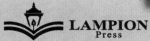